American Public Health Assoc.

The Bertillon Classification of Causes of Death

Volume 1

American Public Health Assoc.

The Bertillon Classification of Causes of Death
Volume 1

ISBN/EAN: 9783337389802

Printed in Europe, USA, Canada, Australia, Japan

Cover: Foto ©Andreas Hilbeck / pixelio.de

More available books at **www.hansebooks.com**

CANADA   UNITED STATES   MEXICO

THE

BERTILLON CLASSIFICATION

OF

CAUSES OF DEATH

RECOMMENDED FOR THE USE OF

REGISTRARS OF VITAL STATISTICS

(After the First Revision of Paris, 1900)

BY THE

AMERICAN PUBLIC HEALTH ASSOCIATION

. AND BY THE

CONFERENCE OF STATE AND PROVINCIAL BOARDS OF HEALTH OF NORTH AMERICA

ISSUED UNDER THE AUSPICES OF THE

AMERICAN PUBLIC HEALTH ASSOCIATION

LANSING
ROBERT SMITH PRINTING CO., STATE PRINTERS AND BINDERS
1899

CONTENTS

THE BERTILLON CLASSIFICATION OF CAUSES OF DEATH.

PREFATORY.

It is with unfeigned pleasure that the Committee on Demography and Statistics in their Sanitary Relations presents this pamphlet on the Bertillon classification of causes of death to the American Public Health Association, and to the official registrars, sanitarians, pathologists, statisticians, and all persons interested in the collection, compilation and practical use of mortality statistics in the three countries embraced in the Association—Canada, Mexico and the United States. Indeed, it will be gratifying to the Committee and to the Association alike if it may be found of even wider usefulness than if confined within the limits of membership of the Association, and it is hoped that it may serve, to some extent, as a means of cementing that world-wide union of registration workers, without which the fullest and best use of international mortality statistics will not be possible.

The time is especially suitable for the general adoption of a uniform classification of causes of death, to the end that the mortality data of the coming century may be more thoroughly comparable than at present. The occasion of the assembly of the public-health workers and vital statisticians of the world at the International Congress of Hygiene and Demography to be held in Paris at the time of the International Exposition in 1900 will afford special facilities for the work of the First International Revision, after the completion of which, and not until then, the classification will be recommended for the practical use of registration offices. There will be only a short interval of delay, as the results of the revision will undoubtedly be ready for use before the end of the year 1900, and in time to begin the compilation of the statistics for the first year of the next century, 1901, thereunder. Indeed, the annual reports for the year 1900 may be so compiled when the work is not begun until after the close of the year, as in some offices.

The Bertillon classification is not presented as by any means a perfect system of classification of causes of death. No perfect system has ever been devised, and should there be, the progress of medical science would in time render it obsolete. As it stands, however, it is believed to be a fairly good working classification, with probably as few serious faults, on the whole, as any other that could be suggested, and a regular system of periodical revision has been adopted whereby the classification can be kept up to date, and also by which the needs of the registration offices of all the countries entering into the revision can be met. It consists of a thoroughly representative method of revision by the practical registration officials, with the advice and help of all students of vital statistics who may be willing to lend their assistance.

It will be understood that the translation of the latest version of the classification (*Extrait de l'Annuaire statistique de la Ville de Paris pour l'année 1896; De la nomenclature des maladies, etc., Paris, Imprimerie municipale, 1898*) is intended to be as nearly as possible a merely literal one, and that the Committee has neither ventured to modify the inclusion of any of the titles to correspond to its present views or to admit any common English synonyms of diseases, however certain their position. This will probably come among the labors of the Commission of Revision, to whom the suggestions of the individual members of the Committee will be submitted in the regular way provided for in the Plan of Revision (see page 34; also page 39).

The most important object to be gained by the adoption of a uniform classification of causes of death is not the mere formal arrangement of the titles employed or the identity of the various groups or classes of diseases. These features are of very minor importance as compared with the precise meaning and comparability of the individual terms composing the tabular list of diseases. It might be supposed that there would be no difficulty in preserving an agreement as to the inclusion of these terms, but in practice this is found to be a very difficult matter. The classification is not intended primarily for the use of physicians in reporting causes of death upon certificates of death. It is not desirable that they should report all deaths under some title of the list. It is only necessary that they should make a precise statement of the cause of death, using any accepted medical terminology for the same, and the translation into the formal list of the statistical table then becomes a matter pertaining to the work of the registration office. This condensation of the multitude of terms describing causes of death, as reported by physicians, into a comparatively short tabular list, such as it is practicable to print in a mortality report, should be governed by the most precise rules, and should be conducted with absolute precision: otherwise terms apparently precisely the same, as used in different countries, states or cities, will in reality have quite different inclusions. The adoption of the Bertillon system affords a precise basis for fixing the inclusion of the terms employed (see pages 18 to 33), and the provisions for revising the classification preliminary to its general adoption with the beginning of the next century (1901), with the co-operation of all registration offices desiring to use the system, and with the advice of all persons interested in mortality-statistics, will enable the meaning of the terms to be settled in accordance with the wishes of the largest numbers.

In presenting this report, which practically concludes, so far as the Committee is concerned, their labor on this very important subject of a uniform classification of causes of death, the Committee desires to express its sincere appreciation of the interest felt in this subject, and the facilities placed at its disposition for use in connection with its work thereon, by the Executive Committee and the officers of the Association, for some years past, and, to join with the warmest sympathy with the members of the Association and with all of the sanitary workers of the country in sorrow for the recent death of our lamented President, Dr. GEORGE H. ROHÉ. May the success of this movement for uniform mortality statistics, which he held much at heart, and upon which the final action was taken by the Association during his presidency, serve as one more token to keep his genial presence before the minds and warm in the recollections of the sanitarians of the country, whom he had served so actively and so effectively in many ways.

Respectfully submitted.

The Committee on Demography and Statistics in their Sanitary Relations.

CRESSY L. WILBUR, *Lansing, Michigan.*
H. M. BRACKEN, *St. Paul, Minnesota.*
CHAS. V. CHAPIN, *Providence, Rhode Island.*
A. G. YOUNG, *Augusta, Maine.*
JOHN S. FULTON, *Baltimore, Maryland.*

✓

RESOLUTIONS ADOPTED BY THE AMERICAN PUBLIC HEALTH ASSOCIATION RELATIVE TO THE BERTILLON CLASSIFICATION OF CAUSES OF DEATH.

At a meeting of the American Public Health Association, held in Philadelphia, Pa., October 26-29, 1897, the following resolutions were introduced by the Committee on Nomenclature of Diseases and Forms of Statistics (now the Committee on Demography and Statistics in their Sanitary Relations) and were referred to the Executive Committee:

Resolved, That the American Public Health Association recommends that the Bertillon classification of causes of death be adopted by all the registrars of vital statistics in the United States, Canada and Mexico, as soon as the change from the systems now in use can be conveniently made.

Resolved, That the Committee on Nomenclature of Diseases and Forms of Statistics be authorized to have printed and circulated among the registrars of the three countries a circular containing these resolutions, the report of the committee on which it is based, the three alternative forms of the Bertillon classification, with explanatory notes on inclusion of terms and practical rules for compilation, and a list of the registration offices adopting the same.

Resolved, That a proposal be made for an international alliance between the registrars of the three countries included in this Association, and the registrars of France and other countries now using, or which shall hereafter adopt, the Bertillon system, and that definite plans for such an alliance shall be submitted for action to the next annual meeting of this Association.

Resolved, That the governments of the United States, Mexico and Canada be likewise requested to make this classification the basis of the mortality statistics of the censuses of 1900 and 1901.

At a meeting of the Association held in Ottawa, Canada, September 27-30, 1898, the resolutions were adopted, as were also the following resolutions introduced by the same committee:

Resolved, That the American Public Health Association approves the general principles and plan of procedure relative to the periodical revision of the Bertillon classification of causes of death as submitted by the Committee on Demography and Statistics in their Sanitary Relations.

Resolved, That Commissions of three members be appointed by the President of the American Public Health Association at this meeting, subject to the approval of the Executive Committee, from each of the countries represented in the Association, to act jointly with each other and with similar commissions from other countries in the revision of the Bertillon classification of causes of death; and that said commission shall be authorized to adopt such necessary rules, in conjunction with other countries associated in the work of revision, as shall be necessary for its successful conduct; they shall report progress to this Association at each annual meeting, and shall be continued until the work of revision is completed and their successors selected for the next periodical revision.

Commissioners were appointed under the above resolutions as follows:

Canada.............
- Dr. Emmanuel P. Lachapelle, Montreal, P. Q.
- Dr. Peter H. Bryce, Toronto, Ont.
- Dr. Elzéar Pelletier, *Secretary,* Montreal, P. Q.

Mexico....... ...
- Dr. Eduardo Licéaga, Mexico, Mexico.
- Dr. Jesus E. Monjarás, San Luis Potosi, Mexico.
- Dr. José Ramirez, *Secretary,* Mexico, Mexico.

United States........
- Dr. Samuel W. Abbott, Boston, Mass.
- Dr. A. G. Young, Augusta, Me.
- Dr. Cressy L. Wilbur, *Secretary,* Lansing, Mich.

Attest: C. O. PROBST,
Secretary.

GEORGE H. ROHÉ,
President.

REPORT OF THE COMMITTEE ON THE NOMENCLATURE OF DISEASES AND FORMS OF STATISTICS.

Mr. President and Members of the American Public Health Association: Your committee desires, first of all, to express its sincere regret that the multiplicity of other duties has made compulsory the resignation of its former able Chairman, Dr. Samuel W. Abbott, of Massachusetts, and to hope that his experienced counsel will still be available, so far as his other engagements may permit, in the service of this committee while discharging its duties to the Association. The principal recommendations of this report, it may be said at the outset, especially those relating to the adoption of a standard system of nomenclature, are made possible by the labors of this Committee under Dr. Abbott's direction in recent years.

The time has come when it would seem desirable that this Association should pronounce definitely in favor of a standard classification of causes of death for use in the compilation of statistical reports. The Bertillon system, reported to the International Statistical Institute at Chicago in 1893, seems to have better prospects of general adoption at this time by registrars generally in the three countries represented in this Association than any other, and therefore this Committee submits as its chief recommendation for action by the Association at the present session that the Bertillon classification be declared the choice of the American Public Health Association.

The classification was printed in full in Vol. XX of *Public Health*,* so that it is unnecessary to discuss it in detail at this time. It has already been put into practical use by the governments of Mexico and of the Province of Quebec in their reports, and several states of the United States will undoubtedly accept it when indorsed by the Association. Among those ready for the immediate adoption† of a modern nomenclature are Massachusetts, Michigan, Ohio and Vermont: while all of the states included in the New England Registrars' Association will, it is hoped, conform. Besides the longer classification printed in the volume of *Public Health* referred to above, there is a shorter and an intermediate classification, each comparable with the longer one, so that the needs of cities and of monthly reports from States, requiring less statistical detail, are fully provided for. It is especially desirable that the municipal reports adopt the same classification as those used by the State systems, and it is very fortunate that, owing largely to the efforts of Dr. Heckard, Registrar of Vital Statistics of Chicago, we have a large attendance of municipal registrars at this meeting of the Association for the purpose of obtaining greater uniformity in classification.

It is not maintained that the Bertillon system is entirely perfect, nor that it may not properly be subject to revision after a reasonable time. It is believed, however, that its adoption in its present condition will afford a working basis of uniformity, and lead to general improvement along the best lines. Much energy is dissipated, and many valuable suggestions come to naught, from the utter absence of co-ordination. Working together, with a broad basis of agreement, many improvements will be made by the associated registrars and come into general use that would not be possible if each state and city continues its development along individual lines.

One of the principal advantages to be derived from the general adoption of the same formal classification of causes of death will be the possibility of reaching a

---

* *Public Health: Reports and Papers of the American Public Health Association, 1894.*

† By immediate adoption is meant adoption as soon as the course of compilation of the registration report will conveniently permit.

better agreement on the inclusion of the terms employed, as related to the original returns. It is obvious that in even the most extended classification in ordinary use. there is considerable condensation or "consolidation," as the term is technically employed, from the statements made in the certificates of death. This is well known to all who have been engaged in practical registration work, but is less obvious to physicians and others accustomed to accept implicitly the statistics as finally printed in the reports. Sometimes considerable discrepancies may arise from varying methods of compilation, and the necessity of a uniform code of rules for compilation can only be met by associated action.

Among the practical questions to be settled in connection with the adoption of a standard classification is the treatment of stillbirths. They are not included in the Bertillon classification as used in France, nor is it generally customary to state them among causes of death in the English classification. Nevertheless, both Quebec and Mexico, in their adoption of the Bertillon system, have so far changed it as to include stillbirths in the regular list of causes of death, thus rendering a correction necessary before comparison with the standard form of the classification. It is recommended that stillbirths be separately stated from other deaths, and that, in case it is considered necessary to include them in the classification, they be stated in connection with total deaths, so that errors from inclusion or non-inclusion of the same can be avoided in comparing reports of different countries. Premature births, living an appreciable time after birth, are not stillbirths. and are contained in No. 138 of the list, "Congenital debility, jaundice and sclerema." Here also may be placed deaths of infants occurring a few days (less than three) after birth without assigned cause of death, whose inclusion under a separate caption was proposed at the last meeting of this Association. It will entirely defeat the object of the adoption of a *uniform* classification if each registration office introduces its peculiar modifications of the original classification.

Probably the most efficient method of carrying out the purpose of this Association, should it authorize an effort at this time to secure practical uniformity in the classification of causes of death, is the preparation of a Circular containing the three alternative systems of classification presented by Dr. Bertillon to the Statistical Institute, with the recommendations of this Committee and of this Association, and the indorsements of as many State and municipal registrars as may be able immediately to promise the adoption of the system in their work. This circular should be distributed among the registrars of the three countries. A set of working rules to secure uniformity in the practical work of compilation should accompany the same. It would be very gratifying if this proposed action should lead to a fuller representation of the official registrars at the annual meetings of this Association, with, perhaps, a formal organization for the discussion of questions of vital statistics and the settlement of practical details of registration. They might well meet as a section of the general body.

There are many States wherein efficient registration of deaths will be impossible for many years to come on account of the great sparseness of population. The sanitary authorities in such States should not be deprived of the benefit of reliable vital statistics, so far as the General Government can reasonably undertake to supply the want. At every United States census since 1850, vital statistics have been collected for such States in this country, but the results, under the discredited method of enumeration, have been imperfect and even misleading in many cases. It is possible to obtain accurate vital statistics of representative areas in all of the non-registration States of this country, which, while not wholly exhaustive, will be invaluable for many important sanitary and sociological uses. The collection of useful vital statistics by the United States Census necessarily implies a permanent organization, such data requiring continuous collection from year to year. This Committee earnestly recommends that the Association exert its influence for the passage of a law by the approaching session of Congress to provide for a permanent census organization, and as an especially important feature of such a law, having a direct bearing upon successful public health work, to provide for the continuous collection of vital statistics in representative areas of non-registration States during intercensal years.

Under the head of forms of statistics, it may be said that the adoption of a standard classification of causes of death, as recommended in the preceding part of this report, will pave the way for many reforms of value in our methods of presenting vital data. It is especially urged that greater attention be paid to establishing a suitable basis of population in the statement of death rates from the common infectious diseases, such as diphtheria, scarlet fever, and others, whose chief incidence is upon a special age class of the population. Rates, as a rule, should be based only upon susceptible population. Similar precautions are necessary in the statement of death rates from all causes, a difficulty which the system of mortality indices, devised by Körösi and adopted by the International Statistical Institute, has been employed to obviate. It is not expedient to enter into the discussion of these subjects in the present report, whose chief object has been to suggest measures whereby the general condition of the collection of vital statistics could be improved, and data of fundamental importance be rendered comparable. Greater exactness and refinement of methods will properly come later on.

Respectfully submitted,

CRESSY L. WILBUR, *Michigan.*
JESUS E. MONJARÁS, *San Luis Potosi, Mexico.*
ELZÉAR PELLETIER, *Province of Quebec.*
A. G. YOUNG, *Maine.*
RICHARD H. LEWIS, *North Carolina.*

ABSTRACT OF DR. J. BERTILLON'S REPORT UPON NOMENCLATURE OF DISEASES AND CAUSES OF DEATH TO THE INTERNATIONAL STATISTICAL INSTITUTE AT CHICAGO, 1893.

The International Statistical Institute, at its session of October 2, 1891, at Vienna, entrusted to us the duty of preparing for the next session a nomenclature of the causes of death. One of the authors of this proposition (Dr. Guillaume) expressed the wish (which he did not think necessary to incorporate in the report which was adopted) that two or three plans should be presented, one of which should be a *résumé* or condensed form of the others, so that each authority might choose a nomenclature more or less condensed without sacrificing exactness of international comparisons. The subject is by no means new.

Already, in 1853, the Statistical Congress at Brussels had decided that it was advisable to "formulate a uniform nomenclature of the causes of death" and had authorized D'Espine of Geneva and Dr. Farr to present a plan of nomenclature at the next congress. In 1855 each of these two distinguished physicians reported plans founded upon very different principles.

In the committee where these two systems of nomenclature were discussed, the president, M. Rayer, called attention to the fact that the classification of diseases was a matter of secondary importance, and that the main point was to prepare a list of separate diseases (*unités morbides*) which were of sufficiently frequent occurrence to merit the attention of the statistician, so that the summary of the causes of death when tabulated by separate diseases or units should always render the comparison of data possible.

It was, therefore, from this judicious point of view that the list drawn up in this manner was presented for the approval of the congress. This list was translated into English by Dr. Farr, into German by M. Virchow, into Italian by M. Bertini, and into Swedish by M. Berg.

The single diseases defined by the congress of 1855 still exist in almost all systems of nomenclature, but do not follow the classification adopted by the congress. We find that the committee, with good reason, attached but little importance to this classification. Today, as well as in 1855, the nature of diseases is too little understood for us to attempt to decide upon a natural classification of diseases. If we pretend to do this, the progress of medical science would completely upset our work, to the great injury of statistics, to which uniformity and continuity are very essential conditions.

Must it then be said that classification is of no use, and that we must be contented with a mere alphabetical list? No, an alphabetical order is an extremely faulty method of classification, and of little practical use, since the greater part of diseases have many names; the reader being unable to tell whether *dothinenteritis*, for example, has been entered under the name of typhoid fever or mucous fever, or of continued fever, etc., would be obliged to read through the entire list in order to find the term. A classification by analogy, therefore, while very defective, is still preferable to an alphabetical list.

Most of the nomenclatures now in use are derived more or less directly from that of Dr. Farr, in which diseases are classed, for the most part, according to their anatomical seat, and not according to their nature. This is evidently right, since the progress of science constantly modifies the opinions of physicians as to the nature of diseases, and consequently, a statistical nomenclature should be modified with the least possible frequency in order to admit of comparison with those of earlier date.

The diseases of each system of organs are grouped together; for example, the nervous system, the circulatory, the respiratory, the digestive, the genito-urinary, the affections of the skin, and those of the organs of locomotion (the bones, joints, muscles).

Besides these diseases, the seat of which is known, there are others which involve the whole organism: formerly these general diseases were separated into several subdivisions, which today are out of date. It is better to group these diseases together, placing at the head of the list those to which Dr. Farr gave the fortunate title of "zymotic;" then those which are termed "virulent:" finally, other general diseases and slow poisons. But it would doubtless be a mistake to make these distinctions in a new nomenclature, since we can today foresee that they will soon lose the importance which was once attached to them. For example, at the present day the list of diseases called infectious includes additional diseases which were once classed under other titles. It is better, then, to avoid these classifications which are necessarily only provisional, and are also useless for statistical purposes.

As many of the speakers at the statistical congress at Paris, and other distinguished authorities have said, the important point in medical statistics consists in the presentation of the relative figures for a certain number of definite diseases.. With the same intent, the authors of the Italian nomenclature have omitted all the titles of general groups. However much we may approve the motive which actuated them, we maintain some of the general titles for the sake of facilitating scientific research.

The preceding statement explains why, in the compilation of the abridged nomenclatures, we were not concerned about general titles covering a group of diseases. We believe that, in the present state of medical science, we should not attempt to establish a definite grouping of diseases. What significance can be attached today to the terms "enthetic, dictic. diathetic" diseases which Dr. Farr proposed for the adoption of the statistical congress of 1855? They have lost all their meaning, and a statistical system which informs us today, for example, how many persons died of "diathetic diseases" conveys but little meaning. But if the name of the group or subdivision has lost its meaning, the name of the separate disease still preserves its significance: for example, this group of diseases, the "diathetic," was made up of gout, anemia, cancer, and senile gangrene. These diseases which seem to us today so grotesquely associated, when considered separately, still preserve very definitely the meaning which they had in 1855.

The history of the past should be our light in the future. Those disease groups which once seemed most natural have rapidly lost their alleged value. We cannot, then, employ them in medical statistics if we aim at permanent work. On the contrary, the meaning of separate diseases changes much more slowly.

It is for this reason, then, that when we compile abbreviated nomenclatures, we shall not attempt to bring together (under a generic term) several diseases which seem to us to be related to one another since we may fear that in a very few years this grouping may become artificial and out of accord with the progress of medical science. It appears much preferable for us to retain, in an abridged nomenclature, those definite diseases which are most worthy of study, partly on account of their transmissible nature and especially on account of their frequency.

RULES TO BE OBSERVED IN DOUBTFUL CASES.

The following are the general rules which we have adopted for the solution of certain difficulties (most frequently caused by incomplete diagnosis, notably in the hospitals):

I. Incomplete Diagnosis.

1. It is not the duty of a statistical office to interpret diagnosis (that is to say, to guess at what has been left incomplete). It can only register facts as they are formulated.

2. When an organ affected with disease is not specified, the certificate should be entered under the title "other organs."

Example.—If the physician writes as cause of death "cancer," without specifying the organ attacked, the certificate should be classed under the title of "cancer of other organs" (25 G).

3. An operation upon an organ (without specification of the cause which has necessitated the operation) leads us to suppose that the organ was diseased. Consequently, for lack of better information, a certificate in which the only cause of death noted is an operation upon an organ, should be recorded under the title "other diseases of this organ."

Example.—Hysterotomy, given as a cause of death without other and more definite information implies a diseased uterus. Hence the certificate which conveys this information should be classed under the title "other diseases of the uterus" (112).

II. Doubtful Diagnosis.

1. In doubtful cases, greater importance is attached to the seat of the disease than to its nature.

Example.—For "abscess of the prostate" there is no special title: it should be classed under "diseases of the prostate" (104) and not under "abscess" (128).

2. The presence of a foreign body in an organ should be considered as a disease of that organ.

Example.—A foreign body in the bladder given as a cause of death should be classed under the title "diseases of the bladder" (102). Nevertheless, a "foreign body in the larynx" or in the "trachea" is to be considered as a cause of death by violence, and should be classed under that title (152).

III. Choice Between Two Simultaneous Diagnoses.

Another question remains to be decided. It very often happens that two diseases are named at the same time as the causes of death: to which of these causes should the deaths be attributed? The following rules are presented to solve this question:

1. When death is attributed simultaneously to two diseases, it should first be ascertained whether one is not a complication. If this is found to be the case, then the death must be classified under the primary cause.

Examples.—Measles and convulsions, compile as measles; measles and broncho-pneumonia, compile as measles; scarlet fever and diphtheria, compile as scarlet fever; scarlet fever and nephritis compile as scarlet fever; scarlet fever and eclampsia, compile as scarlet fever; diabetes and bronchitis, compile as diabetes; typhoid fever and pulmonary congestion, compile as typhoid fever; whooping cough and pneumonia, compile as whooping cough; cerebral hemorrhage and hemiplegia compile as cerebral hemorrhage; felon and purulent infection, compile as felon.

2. If it is not absolutely certain (as in the preceding cases) that one of these diseases is the result of the other, the question should be settled whether there is not a considerable difference in the severity of the two diseases, and then the death should be recorded under the title of the more dangerous disease.

Examples.—Cirrhosis and fracture of the leg. One of these diseases [causes of death] is not the cause of the other. Cirrhosis being fatal, and fracture of the leg only exceptionally so, the death should be recorded as cirrhosis. A still more puzzling example : measles and phthisis. There is no proof that measles has been the cause of a given case of phthisis (although it may have hastened its progress). Phthisis being a more severe disease than measles, the death should be recorded under the title "phthisis." This second example shows that the rule occasions some difficulties. The following suggestions may be adopted in certain doubtful cases : Deaths recorded as from measles and diphtheria, compile as diphtheria; measles and smallpox, compile as smallpox; measles and whooping cough, compile as measles; apoplexy and senile debility, compile as apoplexy; heart disease and softening of the brain, compile as heart disease ; cancer and pulmonary phthisis, compile as cancer.

3. If the two causes of death are equally fatal, and neither appears to be caused by the other, the death should be recorded under that title which describes the case with the greatest accuracy. Generally it is the more rare disease, and this is the name which the physician usually writes first.

Example.—Diabetes and tuberculosis, compile under diabetes.

THREE NOMENCLATURES OF DISEASES.

(Causes of Death.—Causes of Incapacity for Labor.)

FIRST NOMENCLATURE.	SECOND NOMENCLATURE.	THIRD NOMENCLATURE.
	I. General Diseases.	I. General Diseases.
1. Typhoid fever.	1. Typhoid fever.	1. Typhoid fever. 2. Typhus. 3. Scurvy.
2. Smallpox. 3. Measles. 4. Scarlet fever. 5. Whooping cough. 6. Diphtheria and croup.	2. Smallpox. 3. Measles. 4. Scarlet fever. 5. Whooping cough. 6. Diphtheria and croup. 7. Influenza. 8. Miliary fever.	4. Smallpox. 5. Measles. 6. Scarlet fever. 7. Whooping cough. 8. Diphtheria and croup. 9. Influenza. 10. Miliary fever.
7. Asiatic cholera.	9. Asiatic cholera. 10. Cholera nostras.	11. Asiatic cholera. 12. Cholera nostras.
8. Other epidemic diseases.	11. Other epidemic diseases.	13. Other epidemic diseases. A. Yellow fever. B. Pest. C. Mumps. D. Others.
	12. Pyemia and septicemia.	14. Pyemia and septicemia. 15. Glanders and farcy. 16. Anthrax. 17. Rabies. 18. Relapsing fever.
	13. Intermittent fever and malarial cachexia.	19. Intermittent fever. 20. Malarial cachexia.
	14. Pellagra.	21. Pellagra.
9. Tuberculosis of the lungs. 10. Tuberculosis of the meninges. 11. Other tuberculosis.	15. Tuberculosis. { A. Of the lungs. B. Of the meninges. C. Of the peritoneum. D. Of the skin. E. Other organs or general.	22. Tuberculosis. { A. Of the lungs. B. Of the meninges. C. Of the peritoneum. D. Of the skin. E. Of other organs. F. General.
	16. Scrofula. 17. Syphilis.	23. Scrofula. 24. Syphilis.
12. Cancer.	18. Cancer. { A. Of the mouth. B. Of the stomach, liver. C. Of the intestines, rectum. D. Of the female genital organs. E. Of the breast. F. Others.	25. Cancer. { A. Of the mouth. B. Of the stomach, liver. C. Of the intestines, rectum. D. Of the female genital organs. E. Of the breast. F. Of the skin. G. Others.
	19. Rheumatism and gout.	26. Rheumatism. 27. Gout.
	20. Diabetes.	28. Diabetes. 29. Exophthalmic goitre. 30. Addison's disease. 31. Leukemia.
[13. *Anemia, chlorosis.*]	21. Anemia, chlorosis. 22. Other general diseases. 23. Alcoholism (acute or chronic). 24. Lead poisoning and other chronic poisonings of occupations. 25. Other chronic poisonings.	32. Anemia, chlorosis. 33. Other general diseases. 34. Alcoholism (acute or chronic). 35. Lead poisoning. 36. Other chronic poisonings of occupations. 37. Other chronic poisonings.

Diseases are printed in *italics* which appear in statistics of causes of *sickness*, but not of *causes of death*.

Three Nomenclatures of Diseases.—Continued.

FIRST NOMENCLATURE.	SECOND NOMENCLATURE.	THIRD NOMENCLATURE.
	II. Diseases of the Nervous System and of the Organs of Sense.	II. Diseases of the Nervous System and of the Organs of Sense.
14. Simple meningitis.	26. Simple meningitis and encephalitis.	38. Encephalitis.
	27. Progressive locomotor ataxia.	39. Simple meningitis.
		40. Progressive locomotor ataxia.
		41. Progressive muscular atrophy.
		42. Cerebral hemorrhage and congestion.
15. Apoplexy and softening of the brain.	28. Apoplexy and softening of the brain.	43. Softening of the brain.
		44. Paralysis without indicated cause.
	29. General paralysis.	45. General paralysis.
	30. Other forms of insanity.	46. Other forms of insanity.
	31. Epilepsy.	47. Epilepsy.
16. Non-puerperal convulsions and eclampsia.	32. Non-puerperal convulsions and eclampsia.	48. Non-puerperal eclampsia.
		49. Convulsions of infants.
		50. Tetanus.
		51. Chorea.
[17. *Neuralgia, hysteria.*]	33. Other diseases of the nervous system. { [A. *Hysteria.* B. *Neuralgia.* C. Others]	52. Other diseases of the nervous system. { [A. *Hysteria.* B. *Neuralgia.* C. Others.]
[18. *Diseases of the eyes and ears.*]	34. Diseases of the eyes and ears.	53. Diseases of the eyes.
		54. Diseases of the ears.
	III. Diseases of the Circulatory System.	III. Diseases of the Circulatory System.
	35. Acute pericarditis and endocarditis.	55. Pericarditis.
		56. Endocarditis.
19. Organic diseases of the heart.	36. Organic diseases of the heart.	57. Organic diseases of the heart.
	37. Angina pectoris.	58. Angina pectoris.
	38. Diseases of the arteries, atheroma, aneurism, etc.	59. Diseases of the arteries, atheroma, aneurism, etc.
	39. Embolism.	60. Embolism.
[20. *Varices, varicose ulcers, hemorrhoids.*]	[40. *Varices, varicose ulcers, hemorrhoids.*]	61. Varices, varicose ulcers, hemorrhoids.
	41. Phlebitis and other diseases of the veins.	62. Phlebitis and other diseases of the veins.
		63. Lymphangitis.
	42. Diseases of the lymphatic system.	64. Other diseases of the lymphatic system.
		65. Hemorrhage.
	43. Other diseases of the circulatory system.	66. Other diseases of the circulatory system.
	IV. Diseases of the Respiratory System.	IV. Diseases of the Respiratory System.
	44. Diseases of the nasal fossæ, larynx and thyroid body.	67. Diseases of the nasal fossæ.
		68. Diseases of the larynx and thyroid body.
21. Acute bronchitis.	45. Acute bronchitis.	69. Acute bronchitis.
22. Chronic bronchitis.	46. Chronic bronchitis.	70. Chronic bronchitis.
23. Pneumonia, broncho-pneumonia.	47. Pneumonia and broncho-pneumonia.	71. Broncho-pneumonia.
		72. Pneumonia.
	48. Pleurisy.	73. Pleurisy.
	49. Congestion and apoplexy of lungs.	74. Congestion and apoplexy of lungs.
		75. Gangrene of lungs.
	50. Asthma and pulmonary emphysema.	76. Asthma and pulmonary emphysema.
24. Other diseases of respiratory system (phthisis excepted).	51. Other diseases of respiratory system (phthisis excepted).	77. Other diseases of respiratory system (phthisis excepted).
	V. Diseases of the Digestive System.	V. Diseases of the Digestive System.
	52. Diseases of the mouth, pharynx and esophagus.	78. Diseases of the mouth and adnexa.
	[53. *Angina.*]	79. Diseases of the pharynx and esophagus. { A. Pharynx. B. Esophagus.
	54. Ulcer of stomach.	80. Ulcer of stomach.
25. Diseases of the stomach (cancer excepted).	55. Other diseases of the stomach (cancer excepted).	81. Other diseases of the stomach (cancer excepted).

Diseases are printed in *italics* which appear in statistics of causes of *sickness*, but not of *causes of death.*

Three Nomenclatures of Diseases.—Continued.

FIRST NOMENCLATURE.	SECOND NOMENCLATURE.	THIRD NOMENCLATURE.
26. Diarrhea, gastro-enteritis.	56. Infantile diarrhea, athrepsia. 57. Diarrhea, enteritis and dysentery.	82. Infantile diarrhea, athrepsia. 83. Diarrhea and enteritis. 84. Dysentery. 85. Intestinal parasites.
27. Hernia, intestinal obstructions.	58. Hernia, intestinal obstructions. 59. Other diseases of the intestines. [A. Other diseases of the intestines. B. *Diseases of the anus; fecal fistulas.*]	86. Hernia, intestinal obstructions. 87. Other diseases of the intestines. [A. Other diseases of the intestines. B. *Diseases of the anus; fecal fistulas.*] 88. Acute yellow atrophy of the liver. 89. Hydatid tumor of the liver.
28. Cirrhosis of the liver.	60. Cirrhosis of the liver.	90. Cirrhosis of the liver. 91. Biliary calculi.
29. Other diseases of the liver.	61. Other diseases of the liver. 62. Inflammatory peritonitis (non-puerperal). 63. Other diseases of the digestive system (cancer and tuberculosis excepted).	92. Other diseases of the liver. 93. Inflammatory peritonitis (non-puerperal). 94. Other diseases of the digestive system (cancer and tuberculosis excepted). 95. Iliac abscess.
	VI. Diseases of the Genito-Urinary System and Adnexa.	**VI. Diseases of the Genito-Urinary System and Adnexa.**
30. Nephritis and Bright's disease.	63. Nephritis and Bright's disease.	96. Acute nephritis. 97. Bright's disease. 98. Perinephritis and perinephritic abscess. 99. Renal calculus.
31. Other diseases of the kidneys, bladder and adnexa.	64. Other diseases of the kidneys, bladder and adnexa.	100. Other diseases of the kidneys and adnexa. 101. Vesical calculi. 102. Diseases of the bladder. 103. Diseases of the urethra. [A. *Blennorrhagia (males).* B. Others (stricture, abscess, etc.).] 104. Diseases of the prostate. 105. Diseases of the testicle and its envelopes. Orchitis. 106. Other diseases of the male genital organs 107. Abscess of the pelvis. 108. Periuterine hematocele.
	[66. *Metritis and leucorrhea.*]	109. Metritis. 110. Uterine hemorrhage (non-puerperal). 111. Uterine tumors (non-cancerous). 112. Other diseases of the uterus. 113. Ovarian cysts and other ovarian tumors.
[32. *Blennorrhagia.*]	[67. *Blennorrhagia.*]	114. Other diseases of the female genital organs. [A. *Blennorrhagia (females).* B. *Leucorrhea.* C. Others.] 115. Non-puerperal diseases of the breast (cancer excepted).
	VII. Puerperal Condition.	**VII. Puerperal Condition.**
[34. *Normal labor.*]	69. Accidents of pregnancy. [70. *Normal labor.*]	116. Accidents of pregnancy. [116. *repeated. Normal labor.*] 117. Puerperal hemorrhage. 118. Other accidents of labor.
35. Puerperal septicemia (puerperal fever, phlebitis, peritonitis.)	71. Puerperal septicemia (puerperal fever, phlebitis, peritonitis).	119. Puerperal septicemia. [A. Puerperal septicemia. B. Puerperal phlebitis.] 120. Puerperal metroperitonitis. 121. Puerperal albuminuria and eclampsia.
36. Other accidents.		122. Puerperal phlegmasia alba dolens.

Diseases are printed in *italics* which appear in statistics of causes of *sickness*, but not of *causes of death*.

Three Nomenclatures of Diseases.—Continued.

FIRST NOMENCLATURE.	SECOND NOMENCLATURE.	THIRD NOMENCLATURE.
36. Other accidents of pregnancy.	72. Other accidents of pregnancy.	123. Other accidents of pregnancy Sudden death. 124. Puerperal diseases of the breast
	VIII. Diseases of the Skin and Cellular Tissue.	**VIII. Diseases of the Skin and Cellular Tissue.**
	73. Erysipelas. 74. Gangrene. [75. *Anthrax, carbuncle.*] 76. Phlegmon, acute abscess.	125. Erysipelas. 126. Gangrene. 127. Anthrax, carbuncle. 128. Phlegmon, acute abscess.
[37. *Diseases of the skin.*]	77. Other diseases of the skin and adnexa (cancer excepted). [A. *Soft chancre.* B. *Tinea favosa, Pelada, etc.* C. *Psora.* D. Other diseases of the skin and adnexa.]	129. Other diseases of the skin and adnexa (cancer excepted). [A. *Soft chancre.* B. *Tinea favosa.* C. *Tinea tonsurans, tricophytosis.* D. *Pelada.* E. *Psora.* F. Other diseases of the skin and adnexa.]
	IX. Diseases of the Organs of Locomotion.	**IX. Diseases of the Organs of Locomotion.**
	78. Pott's disease.	130. Pott's disease. 131. Cold abscess, symptomatic abscess.
	79. Diseases of bones.	132. Other diseases of bones. 133. White swellings.
	80. Diseases of the joints. [A. *Arthritis.* B. Others.]	134. Other diseases of the joints. [A. *Arthritis.* B. Others.]
	81. Amputation. 82. Other diseases of organs of locomotion.	135. Amputation. 136. Other diseases of organs of locomotion.
	X. Malformations.	**X. Malformations.**
38. Congenital debility and malformations.	83. Malformations.	137. Malformations.
	XI. Infantile.	**XI. Infantile.**
	[84. *Newly-born; foundlings.*]	[137, *repeated. Newly-born; foundlings.*]
	85. Congenital debility, icterus and sclerema. 86. Want of care. 87. Other diseases peculiar to infancy.	138. Congenital debility, icterus and sclerema. 139. Want of care. 140. Other diseases peculiar to infancy.
	XII. Old Age.	**XII. Old Age.**
39. Senile debility.	88. Senile debility.	141. Senile debility.
	XIII. External Violence.	**XIII. External Violence.**
40. Suicide.	89. Suicide or attempt at suicide.	142. Suicide or attempt at suicide. A. By poison. B. By asphyxia. C. By strangulation. D. By firearms. E. By cutting instruments. F. By drowning. G. By precipitation from height. H. By crushing. I. Others.

Diseases are printed in *italics* which appear in statistics of causes of *sickness*, but not of *causes of death.*

Three Nomenclatures of Diseases.—Concluded.

FIRST NOMENCLATURE.	SECOND NOMENCLATURE.	THIRD NOMENCLATURE.
	90. Fractures, dislocations and other injuries.	143. Fractures.
		144. Sprains and disloca-tions. { [A. *Sprains.* B. Dislocations.]
		145. Other accidental injuries.
	[91. *Burns.*]	146. Burns. { A. By fire. B. By corrosive sub-stances.
		147. Sunstroke and freezing.
	92. Accidental drowning.	148. Accidental drowning.
		149. Overwork and inan-ition { [A. *Overwork.* B. Inanition.]
		150. Inhalation of noxious gases (suicide excepted).
		151. Other accidental poisoning.
41. Other violent deaths.	93. Other external violence. Acute poisoning.	152. Other external violence.
	XIV. Ill-Defined Diseases.	**XIV. Ill-Defined Diseases.**
		153. Exhaustion, cachexia.
[42. *Gastric disorder.*]	[94. *Gastric disorder.*]	154. Fever. { [A. *Gastric disorder.* B. Inflammatory fever.]
	95. Dropsy.	155. Dropsy.
		156. Asphyxia; cyanosis.
	96. Sudden death.	157. Sudden death.
	97. Abdominal tumor.	158. Abdominal tumor.
43. Other diseases.	98. Other tumors.	159. Other tumors.
		160. "Plaie."
44. Unknown or not specified diseases.	99. Unknown or not specified dis-eases.	161. Unknown or not specified dis-eases.

Diseases are printed in *italics* which appear in statistics of causes of *sickness*, but not of *causes of death.*

Some diseases of frequent occurrence rarely cause death. It may be advisable to give a place to these in a *complete* nomenclature of causes of death, but not in an abbreviated one. But they should appear in even a condensed nomenclature of causes of sickness. In such cases, they are given in *italics* in the first and second nomenclatures, but not in the third, or extended list.

[AMERICAN EDITORS' NOTE.—As this translation is prepared solely for use as a basis for revising the classification of *causes of death,* no attention need be paid to any diseases printed in *italics,* and which are chiefly important as causes of sickness. In order to make this distinction clear in the fol-lowing discussion of the inclusion of individual terms, the causes of sickness are cut off by brackets, as well as printed in *italics.* Thus quite a number of subdivisions of titles, distinguished as "A," "B," etc., disappear from present consideration, only the general title corresponding to the list number remaining. A discrepancy (found in the original) appears in the number of classes, or general groups, given in the foregoing and in the following lists. Instead of fourteen classes, as given above, there are fifteen in the following text. This difference, which depends on the division of "General Dis-eases" into "Epidemic Diseases" and "Other General Diseases," is of no practical consequence, since the individual terms of the list, designating particular diseases, are chiefly important.]

EXPLANATION OF THE TITLES OF THE NOMENCLATURE OF DISEASES.

(Third Nomenclature.)

LIST showing the synonyms and connected diseases under each title, with references to the diseases which occur as complications of the principal diseases.

GENERAL DISEASES.

I. Epidemic Diseases.

1. Typhoid fever. *This title includes:* Dothinentéritis; mucous, continued, ataxic, or adynamic fever; abdominal typhus.

This title does not include: Adynamia (154); ataxo-adynamia (154); typhoid pneumonia (72).

Frequent complications: Pneumonia; pulmonary congestion; intestinal perforation; peritonitis; intestinal hemorrhage; sloughing; albuminuria.

2. Typhus. *This title includes:* Petechial fever; exanthematic typhus.

This title does not include: Abdominal typhus (1).

3. Scurvy. *This title includes:* Purpura hemorrhagica; Werlhoff's disease.

4. Smallpox. *This title includes:* Variola; varioloid.

This title does not include: Varicella (13).

Frequent complications: Meningitis; endocarditis; suppuration; albuminuria.

5. Measles. *This title includes:* Measly or rubeolar eruption.

This title does not include: Rubella (13).

Most frequent complications: Bronchitis; broncho-pneumonia, etc.

6. Scarlet fever. *This title includes:* Puerperal scarlatina; scarlatinal angina.

Frequent complications: Albuminuria; eclampsia; edema of the glottis; hemorrhage; endocarditis; pericarditis; paralysis; diphtheria; convulsions.

7. Whooping cough.

Frequent complications: Bronchitis; convulsions.

8. Diphtheria and croup. *This title includes:* Diphtheritic, pseudo-membranous, infectious, malignant, or toxic anginas; diphtheria in all forms and especially diphtheria of wounds, of the skin, of the conjunctiva, mouth, etc.; pseudo-membranous bronchitis; pseudo-membranous laryngitis; malignant laryngitis; diphtheritic paralysis.

This title does not include: Stridulous croup (68); spasmodic croup (68); false croup (68).

Frequent complications: Pneumonia; albuminuria; paralysis.

9. Influenza. *This title includes:* Grip; pneumonia due to influenza; bronchitis or broncho-pneumonia due to influenza.

10. Miliary fever.

11. Asiatic cholera. *This title includes:* Indian cholera; cholera (without epithet; cholera morbus; epidemic cholera.

12. Cholera nostras. *This title includes:* Sporadic cholera; cholerine; every disease (diarrhea, dysentery, enteritis, typhus, etc.) accompanied by the epithet "choleriform."

This title does not include: Cholera infantum (82); antimonial cholera (151); hernial cholera (86).

13. Other epidemic diseases. *This title includes:* Pest; yellow fever; eruptive or exanthematic fever; zymotic disease; mumps; German measles; acrodynia; chicken-pox; and every other epidemic disease not specified in the nomenclature.

This title does not include: Epidemic dysentery (84); epidemic cerebro-spinal meningitis (39).

Note.—Whenever a disease here included becomes epidemic it will be necessary to expand the title so that it may be stated separately.

II. Other General Diseases.

14. Purulent infection and septicemia. *This title includes:* Pyemia; absorption of purulent matter; putrid infection; putrid fever; dissection wound; streptococcus infection of the blood (*streptococchémie*).

This title does not include: Puerperal septicemia (119 B); infectious fever (33).

Note.—Whenever the death of an adult female is reported as having occurred from "septicemia," the certificate should be returned to the physician for statement as to whether the septicemia was or was not puerperal.

15. Glanders.

16. Farcy.

17. Malignant pustule and *charbon*.

18. Rabies. *This title includes:* Hydrophobia.

This title does not include: Sitiophobia (46).

19. Intermittent fever. *This title includes:* Paludal fever; pernicious fever; pernicious attack; remittent fever; malaria.

This title does not include: Malarial cachexia (20).

20. Malarial cachexia. *This title includes:* Marsh or pernicious cachexia; marsh anemia; paludism.

This title does not include: Pernicious anemia (32).

Frequent complications: Dropsy; enlargement of the spleen; cardiac or renal lesions.

21. Pellagra.

22 A. Tuberculosis of the lungs. *This title includes:* Pulmonary tuberculosis; pulmonary phthisis; phthisis (without epithet); phymatosis; tubercle of the lungs; acute, galloping or miliary tuberculosis or phthisis; granulations (of the lungs); pulmonary cavities; consumption; caseous pneumonia; tubercular, bacillary, specific, granular, neoplastic or heteroplastic bronchitis or pneumonia; tubercular pleurisy; pulmonary anthracosis; tubercular hemoptysis.

This title does not include: Tuberculosis (without epithet) (22 F): hemoptysis (without epithet) (77 B); pulmonary hemorrhage (77 B); bronchorrhagia (without epithet) (77 B); apical pneumonia (72); laryngeal phthisis (22 E).

Frequent complications: Hemorrhage; pneumonia; pleurisy; persistent diarrhea.

22 B. Tuberculosis of the meninges. *This title includes:* Meningeal tuberculosis; tubercular meningitis; granular, miliary, caseous, bacillary, specific, neoplastic or heteroplastic meningitis.

This title does not include: Meningitis (without epithet), even for children of early age.

22 C. Tuberculosis of the peritoneum. *This title includes:* Tubercular, granular, bacillary or specific peritonitis; peritoneal tuberculosis; abdominal tuberculosis; tabes mesenterica.

This title does not include: Tubercular enteritis (22 E).

22 D. Tuberculosis of the skin. *This title includes:* Lupus; *esthioméne*.

22 E. Tuberculosis of other organs. *This title includes:* Laryngeal phthisis; tubercular laryngitis; tubercular nephritis; tubercular enteritis; bacillary abscess; tubercular ulcer; tuberculosis of the bones.

This title does not include: Pott's disease (130).

22 F. General tuberculosis. *This title includes:* Tuberculosis (without epithet).

23. Scrofula. *This title includes:* Lymphatism; scrofulide.

This title does not include: Scrofulous or lymphatic blepharitis, conjunctivitis or keratitis (53).

24. Syphilis. *This title includes:* Pox; hard or infectious chancre; chancre of the mouth or face; primary, secondary and tertiary lesions; specific disease; mucous plaques; osteoscopic pains; every disease qualified as "syphilitic."

This title does not include: Soft, simple or phagedenic chancre (129 A).

25 A. Cancer of the mouth. *This title includes:* Cancer of the lips, tongue, roof of the mouth, or of the *velum palati;* cancer of the jaw; epithelioma, carcinoma, or cancroid of those parts; smokers' cancer.

25 B. Cancer of the stomach; of the liver. *This title includes:* Cancer of the esophagus; cancer of the cardiac portion of the stomach; cancer of the pylorus; carcinoma; scirrhus, colloid or encephaloid tumor of those parts; gastro-carcinoma; tumor of the stomach.

This title does not include: Organic lesion of the stomach (81); hematemesis (81).

25 C. Cancer of the intestines; of the rectum. *This title includes:* Cancer of the colon; cancer of the anus; carcinoma, scirrhus, encephaloid, cancroid or epithelioma of those parts.

25 D. Cancer of the female genital organs. *This title includes:* Cancer of the womb; cancer of the ovary; cancer of the vagina; cancer of the vulva; carcinoma, scirrhus, encephaloid, colloid, heteromorphous or neoplastic tumor, sarcoma or epithelioma of those organs.

25 E. Cancer of the breast. *This title includes:* Carcinoma, scirrhus, encephaloid, colloid, heteromorphous or neoplastic tumor, cancroid or epithelioma of the breast or mammary gland.

25 F. Cancer of the skin. *This title includes:* Cancroid (without epithet); ephithelioma or epithelial tumor (without epithet); cancer of the face or cervicofacial cancer; *noli-me-tangere.*

This title does not include: Lupus (22 D); esthiomene (22 D).

25 G. Cancer of other organs. *This title includes:* Cancer of the peritoneum; cancerous peritonitis; pelvic cancer; cancer of the kidney, bladder or prostate; cancerous goitre; thyreo-sarcoma; sarco-hydrocele; cancer of bone; osteosarcoma; cancerous tumor or sarcoma of the neck; carcinoma, scirrhus, encephaloid, cancerous ulcer, malignant tumor, sarcoma, or malignant fungus of these parts or of unspecified part of the body.

This title does not include: Cancer of the esophagus (25 B); cancer of the anus (25 C); cancer of the ovary, vagina or vulva (25 D).

26. Rheumatism. *This title includes:* Arthritis; rheumatismal arthritis; rheumatismal meningitis; abdominal or cerebral rheumatism; rheumatismal vertigo; rheumatismal endocarditis, pericarditis, pleurisy or peritonitis.

This title does not include: Organic diseases of rheumatismal origin (57, etc.); nodose rheumatism (136); gonorrheal rheumatism (103 A or 114 A).

27. Gout.

28. Diabetes. *This title includes:* Glycosuria.

Frequent complications: Pneumonia; carbuncle; gangrene; hemorrhage and softening of the brain; tuberculosis.

29. Exophthalmic goitre. *This title includes:* Basedow's disease; Graves's disease.

Frequent complications: Hypertrophy of the heart; cachexia.

30. Addison's disease.

Frequent complications: Cachexia; ascites.

31. Leukemia. *This title includes:* Leukemic adenitis; leukocythemia; Hodgkin's disease.
Frequent complications: Hemorrhage; ascites; apoplexy; cachexia.

32. Anemia, chlorosis. *This title includes:* Pernicious anemia.
This title does not include: Cerebral anemia (52 C).

33. Other general diseases. *This title includes:* Relapsing fever: auto-intoxication; infectious fever; recurrent fever; virulent disease (without other explanation); visceral steatosis; acromegaly; leprosy; syringo-myelitis; Morvan's disease: myxedema: pachydermic cachexia; general fatty or amyloid degeneration.

34. Alcoholism, acute or chronic. *This title includes:* Drunkenness; alcoholic intoxication; alcoholic dementia; delirium tremens; absinthism; dipsomania.
This title does not include: Alcoholic cirrhosis (90); general alcoholic paralysis (45); atheroma (59) or any organic disease attributed to alcholism; amblyopia from intoxication (53).

35. Lead poisoning. *This title includes:* Lead colic; painters' colic; brain disease caused by lead; lead paralysis; chronic lead poisoning; all diseases caused by lead.

36. Other chronic poisonings of occupations. *This title includes:* Mercurial poisoning (hydrargyrism); phosphorous, arsenical or other chronic poisonings in which the statement of the physician (or in default thereof, the occupation of the decedent) indicates very clearly that the poisoning was due to the occupation. In the absence of either of these indications, the death should be classified under title (37). Phosphorous necrosis is always due to occupation.

37. Other chronic poisonings. *This title includes:* Morphinism; cocainism; chronic ergotism.
This title does not include: Amblyopia from intoxication (53).
*Note.—*See inclusion of preceding title.

LOCAL DISEASES.

III. Diseases of the Nervous System and of the Organs of Special Sense.

38. Encephalitis. *This title includes:* Brain fever.

39. Simple meningitis. *This title includes:* Meningitis (without epithet); meningo-encephalitis; pachymeningitis; epidemic cerebro-spinal meningitis.
This title does not include: Tubercular meningitis or any of its synonyms (22 B); rheumatismal meningitis (26).
*Note.—*When epidemic cerebro-spinal meningitis prevails, it will be necessary to double this title, giving the disease a special line.

40. Progressive locomotor ataxia. *This title includes:* Duchenne's disease.

41. Progressive muscular atrophy. *This title includes:* Fatty degeneration of the muscles; atrophic muscular paralysis; amyotrophy; amyotrophic paralysis; atrophic paralysis; pseudo-hypertrophic paralysis.

42. Congestion and hemorrhage of the brain. *This title includes:* Apoplexy; cerebral apoplexy; meningeal apoplexy; serous apoplexy; cerebral atheroma; edema of the brain; cerebral effusion; meningeal hemorrhage; hemorrhage of the spinal cord; cataplexy; apoplectic dementia.
Frequent complications: Hemiplegia; paralysis.

43. Softening of the brain.
This title does not include: Senile dementia (141).
Frequent complications: Hemiplegia; paralysis; pulmonary congestion.

44. Paralysis without indicated cause. *This title includes:* Paralysis (without epithet); hemiplegia; paraplegia; facial paralysis; spinal paralysis.

This title does not include: Diphtheritic paralysis (8); atrophic muscular paralysis (41); pseudo-hypertrophic paralysis (41); general paralysis (45); paralytic cachexia or marasmus (45); paralytic dementia or insanity (45); paralysis agitans, "shaking palsy," (52 C); bulbar paralysis (52 C); ascending paralysis (52 C); infantile paralysis (52 C); labio-glosso-laryngeal paralysis (52 C): paralysis of the palate (79 A); paralysis of the ocular muscles (53).

45. General paralysis. *This title includes:* General paralysis of the insane; paralytic insanity: paralytic dementia; paralytic cachexia: paralytic marasmus: diffuse meningo-encephalitis: diffuse periencephalitis.

46. Other forms of mental alienation. *This title includes:* Dementia; insanity: mental unsoundness; hallucinations: mania; megalomania; monomania; delusion of persecution: melancholia; lypemania: hypochondria: spleen: nosomania; nosophobia: sitiophobia; lycautrophy; nostalgia; homesickness: andromania: nymphomania: priapism: satyriasis: mental disease.

This title does not include: Alcoholic dementia or delirium (34); delirium tremens (34); delirium (161); uremic delirium (97); apoplectic dementia (42): paralytic dementia (45): choreic dementia (51); senile dementia (141); hysteria (52 A).

47. Epilepsy. *This title includes:* Haut mal; Hercules' disease: mal comitial.

This title does not include: Epileptiform convulsions (48).

48. Eclampsia (non-puerperal). *This title includes:* Epileptiform convulsions (of adults).

This title does not include: Scarlatinal eclampsia (6); uremic convulsions (97): convulsions of young children (49).

Note.— Whenever the death of an adult female is reported as having occurred from "eclampsia" ("convulsions"), without other explanation, the certificate should be returned to the physician for statement as to whether the disease was or was not puerperal.

49. Convulsions of infants. *This title includes:* Eclampsia of infants; infantile spasms: trismus neonatorum.

50. Tetanus. *This title includes:* Opisthotonos; emprosthotonos: pleurosthotonos.

51. Chorea. *This title includes:* Choreic dementia: athetosis; Bergeron's disease.

52. [A. Hysteria.] *This title includes:* Hysteric anorexia: hysteric colic: every disease qualified as "hysteric."

52 [B. Neuralgia.] *This title includes:* Tic douloureux; sciatica.

52 [C.] Other diseases of the nervous system. *This title includes:* Diseases of the spinal cord: multiple sclerosis; symmetrical sclerosis; lateral sclerosis: sclerosis (without epithet); tabes dorsalis spasmodica: hematomyelia; hematorrhachis; myelitis; congestion of the medulla; disease of the bulb: bulbar paralysis; labio-glosso-laryngeal paralysis: paralysis agitans; "shaking palsy": Parkinson's disease: paramyoclonus multiplex: ascending paralysis: infantile paralysis: fatty or amyloid degeneration of the cord or of the nervous system; Friedrich's disease: compression of the cord; cerebral compression; cerebral tumor: neuroma: disease of the brain (without qualification): idiocy: imbecility: cretinism; amnesia; paramnesia: loss of speech: aphasia; affections of the brain or nerves; cerebral anemia: neurosis: tic; *tic convulsif;* contracture: anesthesia; neurasthenia; migraine: vertigo: somnambulism: catalepsy; bulimia; Charcot's disease: Landry's paralysis; symptomatic or Jacksonian epilepsy.

This title does not include: Dementia or imbecility of old age (141); syringo-myelitis (33); myxedema (33): pachydermic cachexia (33).

53. Diseases of the eyes and of their appendages. *This title includes:* Ophthalmia: foreign body; conjunctivitis (including gonorrheal conjunctivitis but not including diphtheritic conjunctivitis); [an extended list of diseases of the eye which it is unnecessary to mention among *causes of death;* the same remark applies to some other categories, which with this exception, however, are given in full.—TR.];

diseases of the lachrymal gland and of the lachrymal canals; diseases and tumors of the orbit (cancer excepted).

This title does not include: Cancer of the eye (25 G); ocular tuberculosis (22 F); exophthalmic goitre (29); exophthalmia (29).

54. Diseases of the ears. *This title includes:* Otitis; otorrhea: catarrh of the ear: hydrotitis; foreign body in the auditory canal; obstruction of the auditory canal: polypus of the ear: inflammation of the tympanum: *vertigo ab aure læso;* Meniere's disease or vertigo: caries of the petrous portion of the temporal bone; deafness; deaf-mutism.

This title does not include: Mumps (13).

IV. Diseases of the Circulatory System.

55. Pericarditis. *This title includes:* Cardio-pericarditi; hydro-pericardium; hydro-pneumo-pericardium: cardiac adhesion.

This title does not include: Rheumatismal pericarditis (26); endopericarditis (56); pleuropericarditis (73); pneumopericarditis (72).

56. Endocarditis. *This title includes:* Myocarditis, endopericarditis.

This title does not include: Rheumatismal endocarditis or other acute cardiac affections occurring during an attack of rheumatism (26).

57. Organic diseases of the heart. *This title includes:* Aortic, mitral, tricuspid, cardiac, or valvular affections or lesions; insufficiency: stenosis; Corrigan's disease: cardiac cachexia; hypertrophy of the heart; dilatation of the heart; cardiectasis; steatosis of the heart; degeneration of the heart: cardiopathy; cardiosclerosis; cardiovascular sclerosis; cardiomalacia; persistent foramen ovale; palpitation of the heart; asystole; cardiac asthma.

This title does not include: Heart affections (undetermined character) (66).

Frequent complications: Dropsy; bronchitis and pneumonia; albuminuria; embolism; thrombosis.

58. Angina pectoris. *This title includes:* Cardialgia; sternalgia.

59. Diseases of the arteries, atheroma, aneurism, etc. *This title includes:* Arteritis: fatty degeneration of the arteries; arteriosclerosis: aortic ectasis; Hodgson's disease: stenosis of the pulmonary artery: aortitis: aneurismal tumor.

This title does not include: Aortic disease (57).

60. Embolism. *This title includes:* Thrombosis (non-puerperal).

This title does not include: Thrombosis (puerperal).

61. Varices. varicose ulcers, hemorrhoids. *This title includes:* Varicocele.

Frequent complications: Phlebitis: hemorrhage; embolism.

62. Phlebitis and other diseases of the veins. *This title includes:* Phlegmasia alba dolens (non-puerperal); pneumophlebitis.

This title does not include: Puerperal phlebitis (119 B).

63. Lymphangitis. *This title includes:* Angioleucitis.

This title does not include: Suppurative adenitis (128); adeno-phlegmon (128); bubo (128 or 129 A or 24).

64. Other diseases of the lymphatic system. *This title includes:* Adenoma; adenopathy: lymphoma: lymphadenoma; lymphatocele.

This title does not include: Suppurative adenitis (128); adeno-phlegmon (128); leukemic adenia (31); lymphatism (23).

65. Hemorrhages. *This title includes:* Hemorrhage (without epithet): ligature of an artery: internal hemorrhage; hemophilia; epistaxis: tamponment of nasal fossæ; stomatorrhagia; cutaneous hemorrhage: hematuria.

This title does not include: Cerebral hemorrhage (42): cerebellar hemorrhage (42); meningeal hemorrhage (42); pulmonary hemorrhage (77 B); hemoptysis (77 B); hematemesis (81); intestinal hemorrhage (87); uterine hemorrhage (118 or 110 according to whether it is puerperal or not); metrorrhagia (118 or 110): umbilical hemorrhage (140); traumatic hemorrhage (145).

66. Other diseases of the circulatory system. *This title includes:* Heart affections (undetermined character); splenitis; splenopathy; enlargement of spleen; splenocele and other affections of the spleen; angiectasis; angiectopia; angioma; erectile tumor; disease of the great vessels; permanent slow pulse.

This title does not include: Affections of the spleen due to leukemia (31) or intermittent fever (19); vascular nevus (197).

V. Diseases of the Respiratory System.

67. Diseases of the nasal fossæ. *This title includes:* Coryza: "cold"; nasal or nasopharyngeal polypus; ozena; foreign body; abscess of the nasal fossæ; adenoid vegetations.

This title does not include: Epistaxis (65); syphilitic coryza (24).

68. Diseases of the larynx or thyroid body. *This title includes:* Acute, chronic, erysipelatous, edematous, phlegmonous, or stridulous laryngitis; aphonia; loss of voice; false croup; spasmodic croup; stridulous croup; edema of the glottis; spasm of the glottis; polypus of the larynx; goiter; thyreocele; stricture of the larynx; laryngotomy.

This title does not include: Tubercular laryngitis (22 E); laryngeal tuberculosis (22 E); laryngeal phthisis (22 E); croup (8); diphtheritic laryngitis and its synonyms (8); foreign body in the larynx (152).

69. Acute bronchitis. *This title includes:* Capillary bronchitis; trachitis; tracheo-bronchitis; broncho-alveolitis.

This title does not include: Broncho-pneumonia (71); specific bronchitis or any other synonym of tuberculosis of the lungs (see 22 A); fetid bronchitis (75); summer bronchitis (76).

Note.—See note under No. 70.

70. Chronic bronchitis. *This title includes:* Catarrhal bronchitis; catarrh (without epithet); bronchial, pituitary, pulmonary or suffocative catarrh; bronchorrhea; dilatation of the bronchi; bronchiectasis."

This title does not include: Fetid bronchitis (75).

Note.—Certificates of death in which the word *bronchitis* is not definitely stated to be acute or chronic should be referred to the physician for an exact statement. When it is not possible to obtain one, deaths of children should be classified under No. 69, and deaths of adults and old persons under No. 70.

71. Broncho-pneumonia. *This title does not include:* Capillary bronchitis (69).

72. Pneumonia. *This title includes:* Acute pulmonary catarrh; interstitial pneumonia; cirrhosis of the lung; pulmonary sclerosis; spleno-pneumonia; pneumonia of the apex; peripneumonia; pneumopericarditis; typhoid pneumonia.

This title does not include: Caseous pneumonia (22 A); specific pneumonia (22 A); bacillary pneumonia (22 A), or any other synonym of tuberculosis of the lungs (see 22 A); pleuro-pneumonia (73); pulmonary congestion (74).

73. Pleurisy. *This title includes:* Pleuro-pneumonia; pneumo-pleurisy; pleuro-pericarditis; pleuritic or thoracic effusion; hydro-pneumo-thorax; pyothorax; pleural abscess; pneumo-pyothorax; hemothorax: thoracentesis; empyema; pulmonary adhesion.

This title does not include: Pleurodynia (77 B); pneumo-thorax (77 B).

74. Congestion of the lungs, pulmonary apoplexy. *This title includes:* Atelectasis of the lungs in adults.

This title does not include: Atelectasis of the lungs in the newly-born (139).

75. Gangrene of the lungs. *This title includes:* Fetid bronchitis.

76. Asthma. *This title includes:* Summer catarrh; summer bronchitis; hay fever.

This title does not include: Cardiac asthma (57); suffocative catarrh (70).

77 A. Pulmonary emphysema. *This title includes:* Emphysema (without epithet).

This title does not include: Subcutaneous emphysema.

77 B. Other diseases of the respiratory system (consumption excepted). *This title includes:* Tracheostenosis; edema of the lungs; pneumothorax; pleurodynia; pneumopathy; hydatids of the lung; pulmonary calculus; abscess of the lung. Also the following, in which the nature of the pulmonary disease is not clearly defined: Organic lesion of the lung; pulmonary affection; hemoptysis; spitting of blood; pulmonary hemorrhage; pneumorrhagia; bronchorrhagia; tracheotomy.

This title does not include: Cancer of the lung (25 G).

VI. Diseases of the Digestive System.

78. Diseases of the mouth and of its associated organs. *This title includes:* Stomatitis: diseases of the gums; epulis; gingivitis; bleeding from the gums; glossitis: diseases of the tongue (cancer excepted); parotid tumor: paroditis; salivary fistula: ranula; thrush; diseases of the teeth: odontalgia; dental caries; staphylitis; staphyloplasty; staphylorraphy.

This title does not include: Cancer of the lips or of the tongue (25 A): chancre of the mouth (24); noma (126): mumps (13); gangrene of the mouth (126); diseases of the palate (132 *or* 24); fracture of the jawbone (143); necrosis of the jawbone (24 *or* 36 *or* 132); paralysis of the velum palati (79 A).

79 A. Diseases of the pharynx. *This title includes:* Ludwig's disease or angina; anginas of every nature (except diphtheria and its synonyms: see title 8); amygdalitis; quinsy; abscess of the pharynx, or of the throat; retropharyngeal abscess; paralysis of the velum palati; elongation of the uvula; pharyngitis.

This title does not include: Angina pectoris (58); cardiac angina (58); scarlatinal angina (6).

79 B. Diseases of the esophagus. *This title includes:* Esophagitis; foreign body in the esophagus: lesion of the esophagus: stenosis of the esophgus (except from cancer); spasm of the esophagus: esophagotomy.

This title does not include: Cancer of the esophagus (25 B).

80. Ulcer of the stomach. *This title includes:* *Ulcus rotundum* (round ulcer of the stomach).

Frequent complicatio s: Hematemesis, perforation of the stomach. peritonitis.

81. Other diseases of the stomach (cancer excluded). *This title includes:* Dilatation of the stomach; dyspepsia; apepsia: gastritis: gastro-hepatitis: foreign body in the stomach; gastrotomy; non-traumatic perforation of the stomach; gastralgia; *vertigo a stomacho læso;* catarrh of the stomach; gastrorrhea: indigestion. Also the following in which the nature of the disease affecting the stomach is not clearly defined: Organic lesion of the stomach; gastrorrhagia; hematemesis: hemorrhage from the stomach.

This title does not include: Gastro-enteritis (82 or 83 according to age).

82. Infantile diarrhea; athrepsia. *This title includes:* Gastro-enteritis or gastro-colitis of infants: infantile enteritis; cholera infantum.

83. Diarrhea and enteritis. *This title includes:* Gastro-enteritis or gastro-colitis of adults; enteritis of adults: diarrhea of adults: lientery; intestinal ulcerations; colitis; intestinal colic; flatulent colic; inflammatory colic.

This title does not include: Tubercular enteritis (22 E).

84. Dysentery. *This title includes:* Dysentery of Cochin China: epidemic dysentery.

This title does not include: Choleriform dysentery (12).

Note.—When epidemic dysentery prevails, it will become necessary to double the title "dysentery."

85. Intestinal parasites. *This title includes:* Helminthes; oxyures; tenia: tenia solium; ascaris lumbricoides; cœnurus; trematoda; trichocephalus: ankylostoma: "worm colic."

86. Hernia, intestinal obstruction. *This title includes:* Intestinal strangulation: intestinal invagination; stercoral tumor; ileus: intestinal occlusion: volvulus: hernial cholera; hernial gangrene. *Also the following diseases and operations for causes not clearly defined:* Hydro-pneumatocele; merocele: sarcoepiplocele: sarcoepiplomphalus; kelotomy; artificial anus; stercoral vomiting.

This title does not include: Laparotomy (without other indication) (158).

Frequent complications: Peritonitis.

87. [A.] Other diseases of the intestines. *This title includes:* Intestinal paralysis; enteroptosis; constipation; stercoral fever; intestinal calculi; intestinal perforation; foreign body in the intestine or rectum; rectitis. *Also includes the following diseases of which the nature is not indicated, and the following operations for causes not precisely defined:* Enterotomy; artificial anus: enterrhagia; intestinal hemorrhage: melena; prolapse of the rectum: stricture of the rectum.

This title does not include: Stercoral tumor (86): intestinal invagination and its synonyms (see 86); typhlitis (95); perityphlitis (95).

87. [B. *Diseases of the anus and fecal fistulas.*] *This title includes:* Proctitis: periproctitis; proctocele; procoptosis; fissure of the anus; abscess of the margin of the anus; anal, stercoral, recto-vaginal or recto-vesical fistula.

This title does not include: Urinary fistulas involving the rectum (103 B); artificial anus (87 A); imperforate anus (137).

88. Icterus gravis. *This title includes:* Acute yellow atrophy of the liver: parenchymatous hepatitis: Weil's disease.

This title does not include: Icterus or jaundice (without epithet) (92): chronic jaundice (92); *icterus neonatorum* (139).

89. Hydatid tumors of the liver. *This title includes the following diseases of which the seat is not indicated:* Hydatid cyst; hydatids; echinococci.

90. Cirrhosis of the liver. *This title includes:* Cirrhosis (without epithet): alcoholic cirrhosis: interstitial cirrhosis; amyloid or fatty degeneration of the liver: steatosis of the liver: alcoholic, or interstitial, or chronic hepatitis.

This title does not include: Organic lesion of the liver (92); hypertrophy of the liver (92).

Frequent complications: Dropsy; hemorrhage; pneumonia; tuberculosis.

91. Biliary calculi. *This title includes:* Hepatic calculi: biliary lithiasis: hepatic colic.

92. Other diseases of the liver. *This title includes:* Hepatitis: acute hepatitis: angio-cholitis; cholecystitis; hepatocystitis; choluria. *It also includes the following ill-defined diseases:* Organic disease of the liver: tumor of the liver: hypertrophy of the liver: acholia; cholemia: icterus; chronic icterus: jaundice: hepatic congestion.

This title does not include: Acute yellow atrophy of the liver (88): *icterus neonatorum* (139).

93. Inflammatory peritonitis (non-puerperal). *This title includes:* Peritonitis (without epithet); chronic peritonitis: peritoneal adhesion; epiploitis: metroperitonitis: pelvic peritonitis.

This title does not include: Tubercular peritonitis (22 C); cancer of the peritoneum (25 G); puerperal peritonitis (120); rheumatismal peritonitis (26).

94. Other diseases of the digestive system (cancer and tuberculosis excepted). *This title includes:* Diseases of the pancreas (cancer excepted).

95. Abscess of the iliac fossa. *This title includes:* Iliac phlegmon or abscess: typhlitis: perityphlitis; typhlo-dicliditis: appendicitis.

This title does not include: Abscess of the pelvis (107); periuterine abscess (107): pelvic suppuration (107).

VII. Diseases of the Genito-Urinary System and Adnexa.

96. Acute nephritis. *This title includes:* Acute nephritis: pyelo-nephritis: nephro-pyosis.

This title does not include: Scarlatinal nephritis (6): chronic nephritis (97): tubercular nephritis (22 B); nephritis of pregnancy (121).

97. Bright's disease. *This title includes:* Chronic, albuminous, interstitial or parenchymatous nephritis; albuminuria; amyloid or fatty degeneration of the kidneys; amyloid kidney; steatosis of the kidneys: renal sclerosis. *It also includes he following indefinite statements:* Uremia; uremic convulsions; uremic delirium.

This title does not include: Organic disease of the kidneys (100): puerperal uremia (121); cardiac albuminuria (57).

Frequent complications: Anasarca; dropsy; convulsions; hemorrhage; cerebral apoplexy; pneumonia.

98. Perinephritis and perinephritic abscess.

99. Renal calculus. *This title includes:* Ureteral or renal calculus; renal colic: nephrolithiasis.

This title does not include: Stone (101); vesical calculus (101).

100. Other diseases of the kidneys and adnexa. *This title includes:* Pyelitis; anuria; renal congestion; *ectopia renalis;* nephroptosis; floating or moveable or displaced kidney: renal cysts: multiple cysts of the kidney: hydronephrosis. *It also includes the following ill-defined returns:* Organic disease of the kidneys: nephrorrhagia.

This title does not include: Hematuria (65).

101. Vesical calculi. *This title includes:* Gravel; stone: urinary calculus: urinary lithiasis; lithotrity; lithoclasty.

This title does not include: Prostatic calculus (104). See also (99).

102. Diseases of the bladder. *This title includes:* Acute or chronic cystitis: vesical or urethral catarrh; cystorrhagia: tumor of the bladder: cystocele: cystopsis: foreign body in the bladder: lithotomy; cystotomy: retention of urine: dysuria: paralysis of the bladder: vesical inertia: incontinence of urine; vesical tenesmus.

This title does not include: Hematuria (65): urinary fistulas involving the bladder (103 B); cystosarcoma (25 G).

103. [A. Blennorrhagia (males).] *This title includes:* Blennorrhea: gonorrhea: urethritis; balanitis: balanorrhagia; balanoposthitis: gonorrheal cystitis: gonorrheal rheumatism; gonorrheal arthritis: gonorrheal bubo.

This title does not include: Gonorrheal ophthalmia or conjunctivitis (53): orchitis (105).

Frequent complications: Bubo; adenitis; cystitis; orchitis.

103. [B.] Other diseases of the urethra, urinary abscess, etc. *This title includes:* Stricture; foreign body in the urethra: urethrotomy; urinary fistula (urethral, urethro-rectal, recto-vesical, vesico-vaginal, or vesico-metro-rectal); urinary infiltration; urinary toxemia: urethralgia: urethorrhagia: urinemia; urethroplasty; urethrorrhaphy.

This title does not include: Urethral catarrh (102); retention of urine (102).

104. Diseases of the prostate. *This title includes:* Hypertrophy of the prostate; prostatitis; abscess of the prostate: prostatic calculus.

This title does not include: Cancer of the prostate (25 G).

105. Diseases of the testicle and its envelopes.—Orchitis. *This title includes:* Epididymitis; funiculitis; vaginalitis: hydrocele: hematocele of the testicle, cord or scrotum; castration (of males); Malassez's disease.

This title does not include: Cancer of the testicle (25 G); tuberculosis of the testicle (22 E); variococele (61): sarco-hydrocele (25 G); sarcocele (without epithet) (25 G); syphilitic sarcocele (24); spermatorrhea (106).

106. Other diseases of the male genital organs. *This title includes:* Phimosis; paraphimosis: amputation of the penis: spermatorrhea.

This title does not include: Variococele (61).

107. Abscess of the pelvis. *This title includes:* Periuterine or retrouterine abscess or phlegmon; pelvic suppuration.

This title does not include: Abscess of the iliac fossa (95).

108. Periuterine hematocele. *This title includes:* Retrouterine hematocele.

109. Metritis. *This title includes:* Ulceration of the uterus; ulcer of the cervix.

110. Uterine hemorrhage (non-puerperal). *This title includes:* Metrorrhagia; menorrhagia; Huguier's disease; *tamponnement* of the vagina or uterus.

111. Uterine tumor (non-cancerous). *This title includes:* Uterine fibroma; fibrous tumor or fibrous body of the uterus; hystero-myoma; uterine polypus; fungus or fungosity of the uterus.

112. Other diseases of the uterus. *This title includes:* Uterine or vaginal catarrh; deviation, anteflexion, retroflexion, anteversion, retroversion, or prolapse of the uterus: prolapse of the vagina; elongation of the uterus; amenorrhea; hypertrophy of the cervix; dysmenorrhea, organic disease of the uterus; hysterectomy; hysterotomy; metrotomy; ablation of the uterus.

This title does not include: Puerperal affections.

113. Cysts and other ovarian tumors. *This title includes:* Ovariotomy; castration (of females).

.114 [A. *Blennorrhagia (females).*] *This title includes:* Vaginitis (in females); gonorrheal rheumatism.

This title does not include: Gonorrheal ophthalmitis or conjunctivis (53); vaginismus (114 C); vaginalitis (105).

114 [B. *Leucorrhea*]. *This title includes:* "Whites": vaginal discharge.

114 [C.] *Other diseases of the female genital organs.* *This title includes:* Vaginismus; vaginal tumor; ovaritis: salpingitis; salpinx; metrosalpingitis; hematosalpinx; pyosalpinx: sterility; aphoria; abscess or cysts of the vulvo-vaginal glands.

This title does not include: Urinary fistulas (103 B); and fecal fistulas (87 B) involving the genital organs.

115. Non-puerperal diseases of the breast (cancer excepted). *This title includes:* Mammitis; abscess of the breast (non-puerperal) cyst of the mamma ; tumor of the breast (non-cancerous or unspecified); amputation of the breast.

This title does not include: Fissure of the nipple (124): fistula of the breast (puerperal or unspecified) (124): cancerous tumor of the breast (25 E).

VIII. Puerperal Condition.

Note.—It sometimes happens that the physician neglects to state the puerperal character of the disease. Hence the following rule is laid down for statistical offices: In every such case in which an adult female is reported as having died of a disease which might be of puerperal character, the certificate of death should be returned to the signer for explanation as to whether the disease was puerperal or not. These diseases are the following: Peritonitis; pelvic peritonitis; metroperitonitis; septicemia; hemorrhage; metrorrhagia; eclampsia; phlegmasia alba dolens; phlebitis; lymphangitis; embolism; sudden death; abscess of the breast.

116. Accidents of pregnancy. *This title includes:* Abortion or miscarriage (death of the mother); hemorrhage during pregnancy; uncontrollable vomiting; rupture of tubal pregnancy.

[**116,** *repeated. Normal childbirth*]. *This title includes:* Pregnancy; childbirth, even when it is not stated that the accouchement took place at a hospital.

117. Puerperal hemorrhage. *This title includes:* Puerperal metrorrhagia.

118. Other accidents of childbirth. *This title includes:* Dystocia; Cæsarian section; rupture of the uterus; metrorrhexia; laceration or rupture of the perineum; perineorrhaphy; placenta prævia; retention or detachment · of the placenta; apoplexy of the placenta; cephalotripsy or embryotomy (adult female); symphysiotomy.

119 A. Puerperal septicemia. *This title includes:* Puerperal fever; puerperal infection.
This title does not include: Septicemia (without epithet) (14).

119 B. Puerperal phlebitis. *This title includes:* Puerperal lymphangitis.

120. Puerperal metroperitonitis. *This title includes:* Puerperal peritonitis.

121. Puerperal albuminuria and eclampsia. *This title includes:* Puerperal uremia; nephritis of pregnancy; eclampsia gravidarum: epileptiform convulsions of women in pregnancy; puerperal tetanus.

122. Puerperal phlegmasia alba dolens.
Frequent complications: Gangrene; embolism

123. Other accidents of childbearing.—Sudden death. *This title includes:* Puerperal embolism; puerperal thrombosis; sudden death during the puerperium; death after labor (without other explanation).
This title does not include: Sudden death (non-puerperal) (157); puerperal scarlatina (6).

124. Puerperal diseases of the breast. *This title includes:* Fissure of the nipple (puerperal); abscess of the breast (puerperal); fistula of the breast (puerperal or unspecified).

IX. Diseases of the Skin and of the Cellular Tissue.

125. Erysipelas. *This title includes:* All erysipelas, either medical or surgical, and whatever its situation; gangrenous or phlegmonous erysipelas.

126. Gangrene. *This title includes:* Mortification: sphacelus; gangrene—dry, senile or of the extremities; gangrene of the mouth: gangrene of the vulva, etc.; noma; Raynaud's disease.
This title does not include: Gangrene of the lungs (75); hernial gangrene (86); gangrenous erysipelas (126).

127. Carbuncle. *This title includes:* Furuncle; Biskra's boil or button.

128. Phlegmon, acute abscess. *This title includes:* Abscess (without epithet); phlegmonous tumor: adeno-phlegmon; suppurative adenitis; bubo (without epithet); suppurating bubo; diffuse phlegmon: panaris; paronychia: mediastinal abscess; pus cavity (without other indication).
This title does not include: Bacillary abscess (22 D); abscess of the pharynx, throat or retropharyngeal abscess (79 A); abscess of the liver (92); abscess of the iliac fossa (95); pelvic abscess (107); abscess of the prostate (104); urinary abscess (103 B); periuterine abscess (107); non-puerperal abscess of the breast (115); puerperal abscess of the breast (124); cold abscess (131); symptomatic abscess (131); ossifluent abscess (131); angioleucitis (63).

129 [A. *Soft chancre.*] *This title includes: Chancrelle;* chancroid; simple chancre; phagedenic chancre; bubo from soft chancre: bubo from absorption, or venereal, virulent or phagedenic bubo.
This title does not include: Infectious or syphilitic chancre or bubo (24); chancre of the mouth (24); scrofulous bubo (23): suppurating bubo (128); bubo (without epithet) (128).

129 [B. *Tinea favosa.*]
129 [C. *Tinea tonsurans. trichophy'osis.*] *This title includes:* Tinea (without epithet).
129 [D. *Pelada.*]
129 [E. *Psora.*]
129 [F.] *Other diseases of the skin and adnexa. This ti le includes:* Erythema: urticaria; prurigo; phthiriasis; lichen; pityriasis; psoriasis; dermatitis: eczema: impetigo; herpes; ecthyma: elephantiasis; pachydermia: polysarcia: keloid: mycosis fungoides; seborrhea: trophoneuroses; herpes zoster; Wurdrop's disease.
This title does not include: Pachydermic cachexia (33).

X. Diseases of the Organs of Locomotion.

130.   Pott's disease. *This title includes:* Caries of the vertebræ: spine disease: vertebral polyarthritis.
Frequent complications: Cold abscess; paraplegia; visceral tuberculosis.
131.   Cold abscess; symptomatic abscess. *This title includes:* Ossifluent abscess.
132.   Other diseases of the bones. *This title includes:* Periostitis; osteitis; osteo-periostitis: osteo-myelitis; caries; necrosis; sequestra: perforation of the palatine arch; necrosis of the maxillary bone (not from phosphorus or without indication): exostosis (without epithet): osteoma; bony tumor; tumor of the skull: foreign body in the frontal or other sinuses; mastoiditis; abscess of the frontal sinus, maxillary sinus, etc.; osteomalacia: softening of bones; rachitis; scoliosis; lordosis; kyphosis.
This title does not include: Caries of the petrous portion of the temporal bone (53): dental caries (78): osteoscopic pains (24); osteosarcoma (25 G); necrosis due to phosphorous (36).
133.   White swellings. *This ti le includes:* Articular fungosity; coxalgia: scapulalgia.
134 [A. *Arthritis.*] *This ti:le includes:* Polyarthritis (not of the vertebræ): arthropyosis.
134 [B.]   Other diseases of the joints. *This title includes:* Hydrarthrosis: foreign body in joint: arthrodynia: arthrophytosis; ankylosis; arthralgia: arthrocele: genu valgum.
This title does not include: Rheumatismal arthritis (26): arthritis (20).
135.   Amputation. *This ti le includes:* Only cases in which the cause (of the amputation) is not indicated.
This title does not include: Amputation of the breast (115); amputation of the penis (106).
Frequent complications: Septicemia; erysipelas; tetanus; hemorrhage.
136.   Other diseases of the organs of locomotion. *This title includes:* Hygroma: perichondritis: disarticulation; tarsalgia; painful clubfoot; retracted digits; Dupuytren's disease: nodular rheumatism: rupture of muscle; muscular diastasis: myodiastasis: rupture of tendon: diseases of tendons: tenophyte; teno-synovitis; tenotomy; tenorrhaphy; torticollis; lumbago.

XI. Malformations.

137.   Malformations. *This title includes:* Malformation; monstrosity: anomaly; arrested development; hydrocephalus: megalocephalus; hydrorrhachis; spina bifida: anencephalus: encenphalocele; podencephalus; congenital eventration; omphalocele: exomphalus; ectopia; imperforate anus, etc.: harelip; anaspadias; hypospadias;

cryptorchidism; vascular nevus: polydactylism: syndactylism; clubfoot: talipes varus,. valgus or equinus.

This title does not include: Persistent foramen ovale (57); coloboma (53); painful clubfoot (136).

XII. Infancy.

137, *repeated.* **Newly-born, in maternities—no special disease.**

138. Congenital debility, icterus and sclerema. *This title includes:* Premature birth: atrophy (infantile); icterus or hepatitis of the newly-born; atelectasis of the newly-born; edema of the newly-born.

139. Want of care.

140. Other diseases peculiar to infancy. *This title includes:* Umbilical hemorrhage.

XIII. Old Age.

141. Senile debility. *This title includes:* Senility: old age: cachexia (of the aged); senile exhaustion; senile dementia.

This title does not include: Senile gangrene (126).

XIV. Violence.

Note.—Among suicides should be classed only cases which are definitely stated as such, or which result from suicidal attempts.

External or internal lesions caused by sulphuric acid or other corrosive substances are not classed under poisoning but under burns.

142 A. Suicide by poison. *This title includes:* Voluntary poisoning.

This title does not include: Morphinism (37); cocainism (37); wilful taking of sulphuric acid or any other corrosive acid (142 I).

142 B. Suicide by asphyxia. *This title includes:* Suicide by vapor of charcoal.

142 C. Suicide by strangulation. *This title includes:* Hanging.

142 D. Suicide by drowning.

142 E. Suicide by firearms.

142 F. Suicide by cutting instruments.

142 G. Suicide by precipitation from a height.

142 H. Suicide by crushing.

142 I. Other suicides. *This title includes:* Wilful taking of sulphuric acid or of any other very corrosive substance.

143. Fractures.

144 [A. *Sprains.*] *This title includes:* Sprain; distension of the ligaments.

144 [B.] **Dislocations.** *This title includes:* Luxation; subluxation.

145. Accidental injury. *This title includes:* Contusion; bite (not venomous or virulent); crushing; railroad accident (suicides excepted): injury by cutting instrument (without evidence of suicide); accidental fall: concussion of the brain: perforation of the skull; traumatic hemorrhage: traumatic fever: traumatic eventration: perforation of the abdomen or chest; every acute affection qualified as "traumatic"; wounds by firearms.

146 A. Burning by fire. *This title does not include:* Conflagration.

146 B. Burning by corrosive substances. *This title includes:* Burning by vitriol; accidental taking of sulphuric acid.

147. Sunstroke and freezing.

This title does not include: Cold (newly-born) (139).

148. Accidental drowning. *This title inclu tes:* Drowning without evidence of suicide.

149 [A. *Overwork.*] *This title includes:* Fatigue.

149 [B.] Inanition. *This title includes:* Hunger; insufficient food (not incl uding newly-born); want.

This title does not include: Want of care (newly-born) (139): insufficient nourishment (newly-born) (139); sitiophobia (46); hysteric anorexia (52 A).

150. Inhalation of noxious gases (not suicidal). *This title includes:* Accidental asphyxia (excluding pathological asphyxia and suicidal asphyxia); asphyxia by illuminating gas; asphyxia by stove (fixed or movable); oxide of carbon; conflagation; ammonium sulphydrate; night-soil collectors' lead fumes; chloroform; nitrogen protoxide.

This title does not include: Asphyxia (without other indication) (156).

151. Other accidental poisoning. *This title includes:* Poisoning—criminal, accidental or by cause unknown; antimonial cholera; acute ergotism; absorption of venom; snake-bite.

This title does not include: Accidental taking of sulphuric acid or other corrosive substances (146 B); chronic lead poisoning (35); mercurial poisoning (36 or 37, as the case requires); morphinism, chronic ergotism, etc. (37).

152. Other external violence. *This title includes:* Accident (without other explanation); murder; homicide; assassination (without other explanation); ill-treatment (of an infant);' execution; lightning; electricity; foreign body in the larynx; foreign body in the trachea.

XV. Ill-Defined Diseases.

Note—The following titles comprise only diseases not well defined by the physician, either because his means of information were not sufficient, because the malady was not well characterized, or because the physician neglected to formulate a complete diagnosis.

153. Exhaustion and cachexia. *This title includes:* Debility (adults); asthenia; adynamia; ataxo-adynamia; asthenic, hectic, colliquative or synochal fever.

This title does not include: Congenital debility (139): exhaustion, cachexia or debility of the aged (141); ataxo-adynamic fever (1).

154 [A. *Gastric disorder,* **anorexia.**] *This title does not include:* Hysteric anorexia (52 A).

154 [B. Inflammatory] fever. *This title includes:* Algid fever; carphologia; fever of dentition; autumnal, gastric, bilious, or catarrhal fever.

This title does not include: Continued fever (1); brain fever (76); hay fever (76).

155. Dropsy. *This title includes:* Anasarca; ascites; edema of the extremities and general edema; organic disease (not defined).

This title does not include: Edema of the newly-born (139): edema of the glottis (68); edema of the lungs (77 B); edema of the brain (42).

156. Asphyxia, cyanosis. *This title includes:* Dyspnea.

This title does not include: Asphyxia from external cause (suicide, 142 B): asphyxia from inhalation of noxious gases (150); cyanosis from persistent foramen ovale or malformation of the great vessels (57).

157. Sudden death. *This title includes:* Syncope (preceding death).

This title does not include: Sudden death during puerperium (123), unless the "sudden death" is unaccompanied by an explanatory remark, e. g., "sudden death due to diabetes" (24), or "sudden death from apoplexy" (42), etc.

158. Abdominal tumor. *This title includes:* Intestinal tumor; laparotomy.

This title does not include: Tumor of the stomach (25 B); tumor of the uterus (111); hydatid tumor (89); ovarian cyst (113).

159. Other tumors. *This title includes:* All tumors (except cancer and its synonyms) of which the location is not indicated by the physician; vascular tumor: cystotomy; lipoma: wen; sebaceous tumor.

This title does not include: Fecal tumor (86).

160. "Plaie." *This title includes:* Surgical shock.

161. Unknown diseases. *This title includes:* All of the returns of causes of death of too vague a character to permit them to be classed under any of the preceding titles: Coma: collapse; cough; delirium; suppuration; transfusion of blood; trepanning: tympanites; abdominal tympanites; polydipsia; polyuria; pollakiuria, etc., etc.

[**162. No disease.**] *This title includes:* Simulation.

PLAN PROPOSED FOR AN INTERNATIONAL DECENNIAL REVISION OF THE BERTILLON CLASSIFICATION OF CAUSES OF DEATH.

In view of the actual formal adoption of the Bertillon classification of causes of death by the American Public Health Association, the selection of a plan of international revision becomes at once a pressing practical necessity. Immediate action is necessary in the work of revision in order to accomplish the work in the time available. Much will be lost if the revised classification is not ready for use by 1900, so that the statistics of the next century may begin on a uniform basis. The work of revision should be thorough, and the wishes of·all the countries and registration offices taking part in the same should be consulted. No absolutely fixed plan can be adopted at the present time, until opportunity shall be given for extended correspondence with the representatives of France and other countries taking part in the revision. Some general expression of the wishes of the Association, as representative of the three countries, Canada, Mexico and the United States, should ·be adopted, and working commissions should be appointed at once and engage immediately in the preliminary steps of the revision. Such commissions could report the detailed plan acceptable to the different countries at the next session of the Association for its formal sanction, but no time should be wasted in waiting for such action. In short, responsible commissions should be appointed with considerable discretionary power, exercised in accordance with the general wishes of the Association, and they should proceed to the immediate accomplishment of the necessary work, regularly reporting progress to the Association.

GENERAL PRINCIPLES.

1. A regular periodical revision is necessary for every classification of causes of death in order to keep it abreast of scientific advancement in the knowledge of diseases.

2. It is desirable that as many countries as possible signify their adhesion to this system and take part in its revision, which should be completed by 1900 in order that the international mortality statistics of the twentieth century be compiled on a uniform and strictly comparable basis.

3. All countries adopting this system and taking part in its revision should honorably conform their statistics to the resulting code of statistical procedure.

4. It is right that the wishes of countries making the largest practical use of this system should have the most weight in its revision. Therefore, as the registration of deaths is sometimes imperfect or may not extend over the entire extent of a country, the BASIS OF REPRESENTATION (voting weight) of a statistical office should depend upon the number of deaths registered, compiled and published by it in a year, and not upon the population represented.

5. Suggestions for changes are desirable from all demographers, ·clinicians, pathologists, statisticians, sanitarians, and, in general, from all persons making use of mortality statistics. The decision as to the advisability of proposed changes should remain with the registration offices practically engaged.in the preparation of mortality reports.

6. Continuity is very important in statistics, for which reason no change should be made unless imperatively demanded. Therefore, for the sake of greater conservatism, it would seem advisable that no change be made from the methods now in use unless demanded by at least two-thirds of all the ballots cast.

7. While no changes or modifications should be introduced into the mortality tables during the period between the periodical revisions, the Commissions charged with the work of revision should remain in office until their successors are appointed for the next revision, so that any new questions of classification, or disputed points of classification arising in the meantime, may be referred to them for decision.

8. This revision is purely a statistical matter, and will be best conducted by purely statistical methods.

PLAN OF PROCEDURE.

Article 1.—Each country shall have a National Commission of three members representing the central statistical office for the registration of deaths, if any. For Canada, Mexico and the United States, these commissions shall be appointed by the President of the American Public Health Association, with· the approval of the Executive Committee. These commissions shall be first appointed during the year 1898, and new commissions shall be appointed every ten years thereafter, each commission serving until the appointment of its successor.

Article 2.—Each National Commission shall elect one of its number as secretary, and shall issue to all of the registration offices in its jurisdiction a statement of the purpose of this system of international revision, a copy of the Bertillon system of classification as now in use, and request that any desired changes be suggested on blanks of the form provided, and sent to the National Secretary on or before June 30.1899.

Article 3.—The Secretary of each National Commission shall tabulate all of the suggestions received by him from his jurisdiction on or before June 30, 1899, showing: (1) The tabular number of the list affected; (2) the proposed change; (3) the reasons alleged for same; (4) who proposed such change; (5) the individual or joint opinions of the members of the National Commission as to the expediency of such change. This tabulated report the Secretary of each National Commission shall dispatch on or before September 30, 1899, to the Secretary of every other National Commission.

Article 4.—The Secretary of each National Commission, upon receipt of the proposed changes from the Secretaries of all of the other National Commissions, shall add their reports to his own, with the addition of such opinions of the members of the National Commission as may be given on any particular question, and shall submit the whole to all of the constituent registration offices in his country for ballot on or before December 31, 1899.

Article 5.—The constituent registration offices are: (1) The National office, if a country has one central office, as in England, handling the statistics of the entire country; (2) The State or Provincial offices in countries having no National system of mortality registration, as in Canada and the United States; (3) City registration bureaus where there is neither National nor State registration of deaths. The right to vote should proceed in the above order, to avoid duplication, a city being represented only when it is not included in a State system, and a State when it is not included in a National system.

Article 6.—Each constituent registration office shall cast one (1) vote for every thousand deaths registered, compiled and published in its last published annual Registration Report. Fractional thousands shall not be counted. Each office shall mark "Yes" or "No" opposite each question submitted by the National Secretary, and shall return the ballots to him on or before March 31, 1900. If "Yes" or "No" is not marked opposite any question, the office shall be understood as not voting thereon. A copy of the last published registration report of each office must accompany the ballot when transmitted to the National Secretary.

Article 7.—Census offices collecting mortality statistics shall be admitted to a vote for such portions of a country only as are not covered by State or municipal registration offices, and their basis of representation shall be 10 per cent if decennial, or 20 per cent if quinquennial, of the total deaths recorded for such non-registration area.

Article 8.—Each National Secretary shall tabulate the ballots received from his country, which work shall be examined and certified to by the other members of the National Commission, and present the same at a joint session (International Commission) of all of the National Commissions, to be held at Paris at the time of the International Congress of Hygiene and Demography in the year 1900.

Article 9.—The International Commission shall proceed to elect a Secretary, who shall combine and tabulate the ballots of all of the countries on each proposed change, and, after submission to each National Secretary for final review, shall announce the result of the international ballot.

Article 10.—Two-thirds of all votes cast shall be necessary to make a change. All changes made shall be announced by the International Secretary, through the several National Secretaries, as early in the year 1900 as possible, so that the revised classification may go into effect in the year 1901.

Article 11.—The standard classification to be referred to in all proposed amendments is that of the city of Paris for the year 1894, or the authorized translation issued in the language of each country by its National Commission. After the production of a revised complete classification, the several National Commissions shall be authorized, through the International Secretary, who shall consult all of the National Commissions, to recommend various consolidated or shorter forms for use in municipal statistics and for other purposes; also to settle new points of classification or inclusion of terms not determined by the Revision, such decisions to be operative until the points in question can come up at the next decennial revision.

Note.—The classification of Paris for the year 1894 was recommended as the basis prior to the appearance of the last edition of the Nomenclature, forming part of the annual report for 1896, and published as a separate pamphlet in 1898. The latter, which is translated in the preceding pages, should evidently be taken as the standard of reference at present.

PROGRESS OF THE BERTILLON CLASSIFICATION.

The present satisfactory condition of advancement of the Bertillon classification may be seen in the following translation of a circular letter issued by Dr.
Bertillon to European registrars on behalf of the National Commission of Revision
of France. The necessity of uniformity in the statistical treatment of causes of death
is generally admitted. In practice, however, the utmost conservatism prevails, and
should prevail, on the part of registration offices in adopting new systems of classification, for several reasons: (1) the difficulty of making changes in methods of classification in use, which is of no small importance in large statistical offices; (2) the fact
that comparison with previous years of statistics compiled under the old classification
may be rendered more or less difficult. Since changes of classification inevitably
occur under any system, with the progress of science, the evils resulting therefrom
may be minimized by providing for systematic general revisions at sufficiently long
periods of time, and then making changes simultaneously with all countries using
the system. The advantages of reliable international comparisons should outweigh
those arising from the maintenance of the system of a single country in a fixed (or
fossilized) condition for a long period of time, in the course of which it is inevitable
that changes in the acceptation of medical terms will cause more or less serious dif-
ferences of inclusion. Better to admit the necessity of change, and change with the
world at large. This can be done by a frank union of the nations for this purpose, in
which due regard shall be given to the demands of each representative registration
office. Such a program is provided for by the plan adopted for the International
Revision of the Bertillon Classification.

[Translation.]
RÉPUBLIQUE FRANCAISE,
LIBERTÉ—ÉGALITÉ—FRATERNITÉ.
Préfecture du Département de la Seine.
Paris, le — Janvier, 1899.

"*Most honored colleague:*

"I have the pleasure of informing you that the three *nomenclatures of causes of
death.* which I presented to the International Statistical Institute (agreeably to a
resolution of that body), have been adopted by all the countries of North America
(Canada, United States, Mexico), and by some parts of South America, to be put into
effect in the year 1901.

"It is a remarkable success for the International Statistical Institute.

"At the same time, the directors of the American vital statistics adopted a very
wise resolution, to the effect that the nomenclature in question should be revised
every ten years in order to keep pace with the progress of medical science. This
decennial revision will be intrusted to an International Commission in accordance
with a very detailed and very prudent plan, written in English, which I will send
you if you desire it. The Commissions have already been named for the American
countries and for France, which have officially adopted the plan proposed. The
first decennial revision will take place in 1900.

"It is important that it be aided by the advice of all competent persons.

"For this reason, 1 have the honor to send you two copies of the nomenclature,
requesting that you will have the kindness to examine them and send me, before
March 30, next [before June 30, 1899, will be in sufficient time for our purposes in

this country.—U. S. COMMISSION.] any critical remarks which they may have suggested to you. 1 will make them the subject of a report to the International Statistical Institute at the session at Christiania. They will later be submitted to the examination of the International Commission of Decennial Revision in 1900.

"I venture to ask further:

"Statisticians have always attached the greatest value to the uniformity of statistical lists. The decision of the American demographers constitutes a considerable step toward this grand result.

"You may have the honor of contributing in this direction.

"We venture to hope that your administration will adopt the nomenclature of causes of death presented to the International Statistical Institute. This will be the more easy from the fact that the author, in devising this system, planned to make it a sort of intermediary between the different existing systems. It differs, therefore, as little as possible from the nomenclatures now in use in each country. Furthermore, it is subject to revision.

"If you adopt one of the nomenclatures in your tabulations (or if you agree to adopt the same, after revision, in 1901), your administration will acquire the right to a voice in the deliberations of the International Commission of Revision. If your country adopts this classification, it will acquire the right of being represented in that Commission by three Commissioners. It will also have the honor of having contributed to the uniformity and comparability of statistics—that is to say, of having caused the science to realize a considerable progress.

"I have the honor, therefore, to ask you:

"1. To kindly send me before March 31 the observations which the examination of the nomenclature may suggest.

"2. To inform me whether you are disposed to introduce the system (after revision) into your statistical tables.

"3. To let me know, when possible, whether your country is disposed to adopt it (after revision) as a general measure, in common with France, all of the countries of North America and several of South America.

"Kindly accept, most honored colleague. the assurance of my feelings of the highest esteem.

(Signed.)   "JACQUES BERTILLON.

"*Chief of the Statistical Bureau of the City of Paris.*

"*Member of the International Statistical Institute.*'

"P. S. Following is a list of the members now appointed on the International Commission• for the Decennial Revision of the nomenclature of causes of death, Paris, 1900 :

"CANADA	Dr. Emmanuel P. Lachapelle, President Board of Health of Quebec, Montreal.
	Dr. Peter H. Bryce, Secretary Board of Health of Ontario. Toronto.
	Dr. Elzéar Pelletier, Secretary Board of Health of Quebec. Montreal, *Secretary*.
"COSTA RICA.....	Sr. Aragón, Director General del Departamento Nacional de Estadistica.
"FRANCE.........	Dr. Brouardel. Dean of the Faculty of Medicine, Member of the Institute, Paris.
	Dr. Netter, Professor of the Faculty of Medicine, Paris.
	Dr. Jacques Bertillon, Chief of the Statistical Bureau of the City of Paris, *Secretary.*
"MEXICO	Dr. Eduardo Licéaga, President of the Superior Board of Health, Mexico.
	Dr. Jesus E. Monjarás, San Luis Potosí.
	Dr. José Ramirez, Secretary of the Superior Board of Health. Mexico, *Secretary*.
"UNITED STATES.	Dr. Samuel W. Abbott. Secretary Massachusetts State Board of Health. Boston Mass.
	Dr. A. G. Young, Secretary Maine State Board of Health. Augusta. Me.
	Dr. Cressy L. Wilbur. Chief of Vital Statistics of Michigan. Lansing Mich., *Secretary.*"

The immediate adoption of the Bertillon classification, i. e., its actual application to practical use, is no longer recommended (except under exceptional circumstances) until the results of the first revision shall have become accessible. When an office does not possess a fairly satisfactory system of tabulation, or if a new or improved method of registration should go into effect, thereby making a natural division between the former and present statistics, then the immediate adoption of the Bertillon classification might be advisable. But under ordinary circumstances it would be better to wait during the short time now intervening, and begin the use of the revised system with the first year of the next century, 1901. It will probably be ready in time for the compilation of annual reports covering the year 1900, but for monthly or weekly bulletins, its use cannot be well begun before 1901. **The early acceptance of the classification is very desirable,** *however, by all registration offices, so that they may fully participate in the work of revision. Registrars should notify the Secretaries of the Commissions of Revision for their respective countries, or if in countries which have not yet signified their adhesion to the system, should organize a National Commission and notify other countries of their desire to join in the movement for uniform statistics.* Probably the most convenient manner of accomplishing this will be to address Dr. Jacques Bertillon, *Chef des travaux statistiques de la Ville de Paris,* 1. Avenue Victoria. Paris, France, who will supply any information desired.

HOW TO AID IN THE WORK OF REVISION.

The plan of revision may be outlined as follows:

1. Each country participating is to have a National Commission of three members, representing its registration service.

2. *The Secretary of each National Commission is to circulate the Bertillon classification in its present form among the registration offices, sanitarians, pathologists, statisticians, and others interested in statistics of causes of death, and invite expressions of opinion from them as to desirable changes in the present system. They should be received by June 30, 1899.*

3. The Secretary of each National Commission shall arrange and tabulate all of the suggestions received from his country up to June 30, 1899, and send copies to the Secretaries of the other National Commissions before September 30, 1899.

4. The Secretary of each National Commission shall submit the suggestions received from his own country, together with those derived from other countries, to the *registrars* of his country for ballot (only those participating who have adhered to the system) prior to December 31, 1899. A registration office will have weight in proportion to the number of deaths registered. Of course, a country having a national system of registration will vote as a unit. A consensus of two-thirds is necessary to introduce any change. [This method confines the actual decision as to proposed changes to the practical registrars, who can best count the cost of making them, while it enlists the advice and opinions of all interested in vital statistics as to the desirability of alterations in the present methods.]

5. The voting registrars should submit their ballots before March 31, 1900, to their National Secretary.

6. The National Secretaries should tabulate the ballots received and present them, at a session of the International Commission, to be held at Paris in 1900 (the exact date to be subsequently announced) in connection with the International Congress of Hygiene and Demography. The results of the International Revision will be announced as soon thereafter as possible, so that they may be ready for practical use, at latest, by the beginning of the year 1901.

Your Personal Assistance is Requested.

We are at present concerned only with the second step, for which this pamphlet has been especially prepared.

All registration officials, members and officers of State and municipal boards of health, sanitarians, pathologists, statisticians, actuaries and, in general, all who make use of or feel an interest in the subject of comparable mortality statistics are earnestly requested to carefully examine the preceding pages (pp. 13 to 33), showing the Bertillon system in its present form, and to submit a statement of any desired changes, with a memorandum of the reasons therefor, to the Secretary of their National Commission (see list on page 5). This should be done on or before June 30, 1899.

It is desirable that each suggestion, relating to a distinct change proposed, should be on a separate sheet of paper. The tabular number (or numbers) of the list should always be given so that the reference may be exact, and the titles to be changed in full. The reason for the proposed change should then be briefly stated, and the full name and postoffice address of the correspondent should be given. It is desirable that the official title be also given, if any, and any references to statistical data supporting the proposed change may be appended. As an example of a convenient form the following may be submitted :

Transfer 130. Pott's disease, to 22e, Tuberculosis of other organs.

Pott's disease is usually tubercular. Other similar tubercular diseases may well be joined with it for general statistical treatment. All tuberculosis should be together under one general title.

(Signed.)   CRESSY L. WILBUR, M. D.,
                        Chief of Vital Statistics, Michigan.

Lansing, Mich., March 16, 1899.